# King Biscuit

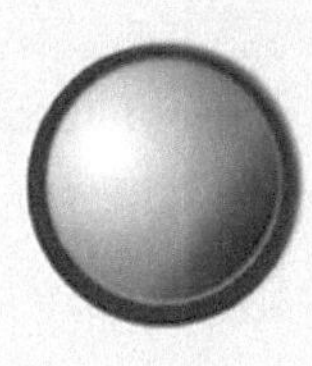

recorded by Michael Loyd Gray

Skywater Publishing Cooperative
Chaska, Minnesota
https://skywaterpub.com



*Library of Congress Cataloging-in-Publication Data*
Gray, Michael Loyd.
    *King Biscuit* / by Michael Loyd Gray.
    p. cm.
    Summary: In the summer of 1966, seventeen-year-old Billy Ray
Fleener sets out on a road trip from Argus, Illinois, to the Helena,
Arkansas, grave of his beloved Uncle Mitt who died in Vietnam,
meeting colorful and famous people along the way and becoming the
youngest music producer ever at a blues festival.
    ISBN 979-8-8691-8996-7 (pbk.)
    ISBN 979-8-879454-59-8 (Amazon pbk.)
    [1. Coming of age—Fiction. 2. Voyages and travels—Fiction.
3. Uncles—Fiction. 4. Death—Fiction. 5. Celebrities—Fiction.
6. Blues (Music)—Fiction. 7. Music festivals—Fiction. 8. Family life—
Fiction. 9. Nineteen sixties—Fiction.] I. Title.
PZ7.G7797Kin 2013
[Fic]—dc23                           2012022903

**Credits**
Blake Hoena, editorial direction
Flat Sole Studio, cover design and book layout

**Photo Credits**
Shutterstock, cover

# King Biscuit

recorded by Michael Loyd Gray

# The Plan

The rumor whispered in Argus, Illinois, that summer was that Margie Heinrich and her cheerleader girlfriends skinny-dipped at Cottage Pond, which was favored for church picnics by day and teenagers guzzling Pabst Blue Ribbon at night. No one actually claimed to have seen young Margie in the buff, but Billy Ray Fleener, a year behind her at Curtis LeMay High School, was hoping. When he wasn't waiting for abrupt boners to subside in his Levi's, he mounted his ten-speed and furiously pedaled out to the pond, which was shaded by a thick grove of Cottonwoods and Pawpaws.

Billy Ray was sixteen but already five foot ten and beginning to fill out. He was considered a good-looking boy, though perhaps some folks felt his sideburns inched too far down his cheeks like fuzzy caterpillars in a hurry. They suggested the potential for impertinence; though that was just idle speculation, and the only impertinent thoughts on Billy Ray's mind concerned the peach fuzz he had once glimpsed on Margie's tan thighs where her cut-off jeans ended and the eternal anatomical mystery began. It was early June, 1966, and so far all Billy Ray had seen at the pond were holy-roller types at a First Baptist Church barbecue.

As a restless boy who sensed manhood was not so far off, Billy Ray had a plan of sorts for easing into it: he fancied going out to California to become a professional surfer. He'd get a cool name, like MoonDoggy (he knew that one was taken by somebody in the movies) or Sharkman. His current favorite was Tubular Boy, and he imagined he would wear baggies and surfer shirts, listen to the Beach Boys, and wax his board a lot in the company of surfer girls in bikinis. He bought *Surfer* magazine at the Walgreen's in downtown Argus and already knew some of the surfer lingo. His favorite surfer expression was "Cowabunga."

But the plan had one fundamental flaw: Billy Ray had no money and no car, and he was still in high school in east central Illinois. The closest thing to surf for him were waves of corn that shimmied and rattled when there was a breeze. California was more a state of mind, a concept or philosophy, than a reality to Billy Ray, who had nonetheless scrutinized it pretty well in an atlas at the school library.

On this particular day at Cottage Pond the picnic tables had been pushed together in a long row to accommodate the ladies of the Argus Flower Garden Society, which was a definite sign to Billy Ray that there would be no Margie Heinrich skinny dipping. Several of the ladies recognized him and waved. Chief among them Mrs. Dobbs, who lived across the street from Billy Ray, and who tended a very colorful garden of marigolds and gardenias. He forced a smile and waved back at Mrs. Dobbs, and as he turned to pedal back to Argus, he heard a hideous commotion erupt—the main eruption coming from Minnie Sullivan, wife of Argus Mayor Hedges Sullivan.

The tables were abruptly emptied of ladies, who all fled to the nearest bank of Cottage Pond, where Mrs. Sullivan was pointing and hopping up and down and basically freaking out.

Billy Ray figured she was just having another of her spells, which usually signaled that she believed herself in the presence of The Lord. But all the commotion turned out to be focused on Mrs. Sullivan's wiener dog—Purdy Boy—who somehow had gotten himself smack in the middle of Cottage Pond.

As Purdy Boy dog paddled in a circle in the pond, Mrs. Sullivan shrieked even louder and all the ladies joined in and made it a choir. They were dressed to the nines, Billy Ray noted, in fine silk dresses and high heels and voluminous hats and white gloves, and he wondered for a moment why they'd put on those costumes just to sit around picnic tables in the grass by a pond, but he had lately given up on understanding why adults insisted on doing everything in high ceremony.

It was Mrs. Dobbs who summoned Billy Ray first, but Minnie Sullivan was also quick to implore him to jump in and save Purdy Boy, who truth be told, Billy Ray thought, looked like a pretty good swimmer. But the little wiener dog showed signs of fatigue and panic. After he slipped beneath the surface once and popped up sputtering water, Billy Ray resigned himself to his fate and kicked off his Converse basketball shoes, slipped off his t-shirt, and waded into Cottage Pond, where by then Purdy Boy had gone under again. Billy Ray got to him just in time.

Fetching Purdy Boy proved to be only the start of Billy Ray's problems because once he'd deposited the scrawny, saturated critter on the ground, Purdy Boy didn't move. He just remained in a wiener dog fetal position. Minnie Sullivan began to pray for her Purdy Boy and all the other ladies conveyed looks of shock so grave as to nearly suggest the ones they had the day President Kennedy was shot in Dallas.

Billy Ray liked dogs and all animals as much as the next guy, but what really motivated him was the fear of riding back to Argus with a wet and smelly dead wiener dog on his lap, and fifteen shrieking ladies, so he went to work on Purdy Boy, first massaging his stomach and holding him up with his head down to drain the water. Finally, in desperation, he opened the dog's mouth and tried blowing into it like his gym teacher had demonstrated mouth-to-mouth in first aid class. He had often fantasized about mouth-to-mouth with Margie, and even practised inhaling and exhaling when no one was looking. Maybe that was what did it because Purdy Boy opened his eyes and vomited some water and something greenish. After a few minutes he was even wagging his wiener dog tail.

Minnie Sullivan insisted that Billy Ray put his bike in the back of Mrs. Dobbs' Rambler station wagon and ride back to Argus with the ladies. Someone produced a towel that had been used to cushion bowls of potato salad on the ride out, and he slipped on his t-shirt but had to ride back with wet jeans and surrounded by flower ladies who kept shooting him adoring glances.

In Argus they stopped at Mayor Sullivan's office, where Minnie regaled her husband with the tale of Purdy Boy's brush with death and proclaimed Billy Ray a hero, to which Mayor Sullivan seconded the motion. Someone asked Billy Ray what he'd like as a reward. Billy Ray remembered that he had a plan to get to California and surf, so he said he could use some kind of job for the summer. Mayor Sullivan said he'd get right to work on finding him one, but on the spot awarded him fifty dollars from the Argus Good Deeds Program.

Minnie Sullivan had Billy Ray and his parents over to her house the next day for lemonade and fresh-baked cookies— chocolate chip. Everyone said his rescue of Purdy Boy indicated Billy Ray was blessed with luck and had a bright life ahead of him. When someone asked him what he wished for in the future, he just smiled and looked down at his shoes, and everyone took it for modesty, a quality much-valued in Argus.

Actually Billy Ray was silent because he was assessing whether his star had brightened enough so he could get into Margie Heinrich's pants.

# 2

# Fleener and Son

Friday afternoon.

Fleener Hardware at Douglas and Lincoln.

Rain fell in sheets.

Dwight Cruikshank compared half-inch bolts.

Ida Kent pondered toilet seats—plain, floral?

Belinda Simmons searched for a clerk.

Mrs. Dobbs fretted by a window and watched the rain.

Frank Palmer eyed a Phillips screwdriver.

Roger Gilstrap admired his new toilet plunger.

Mayor Sullivan waddled down the power tools aisle.

Mrs. Carruthers praised a cashier's wedding ring.

Mr. Fleener sold Mr. Newbury a shovel.

Billy Ray hid from his father on the loading dock and studied *Surfer* magazine when he wasn't contemplating his new status as a local hero of sorts.

Hero.

Mrs. Dobbs had gushed it to everybody.

Mrs. Sullivan, too.

The mayor hailed him as "young man" whenever they met on a street or in a store. People that didn't know Billy Ray at all congratulated him for saving Purdy Boy.

The tale had permeated Argus thoroughly.

But Mr. Fleener hadn't signed on with the Billy Ray Fan Club.

"It's good you saved that dog," Mr. Fleener said. "Lord knows Minnie Sullivan is nuts for it. But even heroes need a job."

And so he put Billy Ray to work sweeping floors and counting gaskets and screwdrivers and mops and brooms and all the other utterly boring things stacked to the ceiling in Fleener Hardware—soon to be Fleener and Son his father had hinted. Billy Ray had felt sick to his stomach.

After just a week it threw him almost into a tizzy, and he was sure he'd lose himself and have to surrender his promising, bright life for an orange vest with a name tag that said Fleener and Son. It was the most dreadful thing he could imagine. Worse even than never scaling Mount Margie Heinrich. It wasn't that Billy Ray somehow was lazy or didn't see the value of hard work, but ever since he could remember, his father had been the Grand Prophet of Republican Values, stressing Devotion and Servitude and perpetuating the American Dream of Hard Work, Sacrifice, and more Hard Work.

It was enough for Billy Ray to pop a gasket. He wanted more. He just didn't know yet what more was. He figured it had something to do with romance. Not the romance between men and women, but the romance Mrs. Withers always got tingly about in English class when they read something by Shakespeare or Hemingway or Fitzgerald. The romance of life was what he guessed more was. Or could be. The romance of seeing more and being more than just becoming the Hardware King of Argus. Billy Ray had glimpsed the world outside Argus in books, on TV, and from firsthand accounts of people who had escaped the gravitational pull of Argus and ventured out into the Great Beyond the Horizon. He longed to sail into the Winds of Chance to see where they deposited him.

Surfing, for example, was out there in the Great Beyond. He'd seen surfers on TV. They seemed to inhabit a watery world of ease and fun and daunting runs down humongous waves. It all struck him as heroic. After work he would steal away to the loading dock alone to inhale *Surfer* magazine. The latest issue featured a two-page color photo, and the surfers were pathetically small dots on a tsunami-like blue wave in Hawaii—the Banzai Pipeline.

Billy Ray knew that the Pipeline was Big Time Surfer Stuff. Surfers from all over the world went there just to experience it. It was the surfing Mecca. The name itself was so Tubular Banzai. What a word. Like the Japanese screamed in World War II when they made suicide charges. He had seen that in John Wayne movies like *The Sands of Iwo Jima* and *Fighting Seabees*.

Billy Ray looked up one day from his magazine and listened to the hissing rain. It had the volume of surf, he thought, though his ability to gauge surf was pure speculation and basically nonexistent, and so his face was back into the picture of The Pipeline—named by a photographer who surfed there and shouted "banzai!" in the 1950s. Billy Ray could just imagine the guy out there on that wave shouting like a tomfool and waving his arms. The waves sometimes reached twenty-five feet or more over a shallow reef, and Billy Ray wondered how often surfers got cut feet from the coral. In biology class he learned that coral was alive and sharp as a razor. He decided that surfers should wear some sort of shoe. Maybe he would introduce that to the sport and become a hero among surfers.

He learned a lot about surfing. From May to September, he read that something called Limu, a kind of seaweed, could sting surfers. Limu? Stinging seaweed? There were sharks, too. And stingrays. And jellyfish. It was dangerous stuff. The worst thing Billy Ray had ever suffered from nature was poison ivy from taking a dump in the weeds along the banks of the Mackinaw River during Boy Scouts camp. That and the catfish that horned his thumb something fierce and drew blood at Cottage Pond. He tried to envision stinging seaweed, but it wouldn't quite make a picture in his head.

The rain drummed harder like a machine gun on the tin roof over the loading dock, but Billy Ray didn't pay any attention. He gawked at the huge waves in the picture. Could he do that? To test himself he'd tried the Tilt-A-Whirl and roller coaster at the McLean County Fair. He rode the Tilt-A-Whirl three times without throwing up. The roller-coaster, he had to admit, was pretty small and tame, but he figured the ups and downs and sudden curves were similar to riding a wave. During the curves Billy Ray twisted and turned his body in and out against the mild G-forces as though he were on a surfboard.

But his friend Moss Newbury said that all the sissy rollercoaster proved was that even pussies could ride it, and besides, Moss added, Mr. Fleener would never allow him to be anything but a slave to Hardware, Mediocrity, and The American Way.

It was all enough to slide Billy Ray into a soggy, irreversible depression, except for a growing but still vague sense that he was destined for more than crescent wrenches and toilet plungers, and that he must resist Gleaming Hardware Slavery until The Answer presented itself, whether that was surfing or even seeing the world as a merchant seaman, though Billy Ray had never thought much about being a merchant seaman. He did think a lot about his uncle Milt, who had been a kaleidoscope of activity, who always spawned fun and adventure and skirted the rules. It was always weird to him to think of Milt as dead. But he was very dead. Deader than a doornail. He had been a slab-faced Marine who was among the first to die in Vietnam.

On a brilliantly sunny day in the A-Shau Valley, cheerful Milt had stepped on a mine made from a stolen American 155mm artillery shell. It reduced his jolly six-foot-three frame to something much more compact while vaporizing five other soldiers, too. But Billy Ray chose to remember Milt as he had been—larger than life—and not what he had been reduced to, a gelatinous mass and splintered bones. Milt had been his life preserver, and Billy Ray had drawn on him many times. Milt rescued him from the dreariness and predictable Bible thumping of his father. That was Milt's phrase, "Predictable Bible thumper." Milt and Billy Ray's father were like night and day, up and down, drunk and sober.

Billy Ray knew a little about Bible thumping from Sunday school. He knew it meant you had to be serious an awful lot and not waver in any of your beliefs, despite the facts, and not laugh when something was funny, and trust God without blinking an eye. And be thrifty, but make money, and take care of property and let people know what's best for them.

After one particularly somber and dry Baptist service and Sunday school, Milt had rescued Billy Ray from the post-church sermon from his father, and they fled in Milt's battered green '57 Chevy out to the Mackinaw River to fish. This was just before Milt joined the Marines. Billy Ray was a ninth grader.

"Don't you believe in God, Milt?"

Milt was watching his red bobber closely. A bluegill, or maybe a bass, he figured, was toying with his bait, and the bobber danced up and down a few times.

"Sure, I believe in God." With his left hand he gently pulled on the line to add tension to see if the fish would commit.

"Why do you ask, Billy Ray?" He didn't look up and kept his eyes on the bobber.

"I don't know," Billy Ray said. "I guess because you never go to church." He looked at his own bobber, but nothing was happening.

"Slip your line between your fingers, Billy Ray. Do it slowly. Don't jerk it. That's how you can feel a fish nibbling at the other end."

Billy Ray did it, but didn't feel anything. "Where'd you learn that?"

"In Arkansas. Growing up in Helena, Billy Ray. When your pappy and me were just whistledick kids peeing in the Mississippi."

Whistledick. Billy Ray loved the strange but funny things that popped out of Milt's mouth.

"Did you really pee in the Mississippi?"

Milt smirked. "Damn straight we did. We mooned barges, too. We always imagined we were pissing on the folks down river in New Orleans. It was funny at the time."

Billy Ray marveled at the thought.

"Was my dad like he is now when you were kids in Arkansas?"

Milt concentrated on the bobber, but it had stopped dancing. "I reckon whatever it was is gone now." He pulled slightly on the line, but there was no resistance except for the constant, known pressure of the current, which was mild. The brown river oozed by them stiffly.

"Was he?" Billy Ray repeated.

"Like how, Billy Ray?"

"Like he is now. Crazed."

Milt glanced at Billy Ray. "Do you really think he's crazed?"

Billy Ray chewed his lower lip and concentrated hard on the question. "Well, you said he was a fundamentalist, and predictable."

"I did. And he is. On both counts." He checked the line again, but felt only the current. "But does that make him crazed? Damn, that sucker is gone. He was pretty interested there for a while, though. I bet it was a wily old bass."

Billy Ray brightened: "Crazed, but not crazy." He looked to Milt expectantly.

"Good for you, Billy Ray. There is a difference. No, your pa was different as a boy. But when your grandpa died, he had to grow up in a hurry, I reckon. After all, he was the oldest. He turned to the church for guidance. Some do, some don't."

"You didn't."

"Doesn't mean I don't believe." Milt reeled in his line. "Just what I thought. That sucker stripped me clean. You know, Billy Ray, church is everywhere. God hears us and sees us right here on this river. We don't have to sit in a pew on Oak Street for that."

Billy Ray was pretty sure there was a God, though it was definitely one of those foggy mysteries you had to take on faith alone and the word of others because proof was slippery and elusive and in church nobody was interested in facts or evidence, just faith. But did everybody have to check their sense of humor at the church door? Were adventure and fun really incompatible with religion? His father made it seem so. Couldn't a Christian be a cheerful Christian? A fun Christian?"

Live and let live was what Milt said was his motto. Billy Ray agreed. There just had to be more to being a Christian than drudgery. What did work and sacrifice and duty add up to if there was no reward, no payoff?

"Did my dad really moon barges on the Mississippi?" Billy Ray couldn't imagine his father dropping his pants and exposing his bare butt to anybody. He rarely even wore open collars, even when it was hot, and he was never without a tie at Fleener Hardware.

Milt remembered and laughed. "We did it all the time. Hell, Billy Ray, those barges were so far away they couldn't see us anyway. It was just a lark—rubbernecking. We didn't think about it."

"What's rubbernecking?"

"Showing off."

Billy Ray nodded. After a while he said, "I might become a surfer. Out in California."

"That's what I hear," Milt said. "California's the place for it alright."

"What do you think?"

Milt shrugged. "I think that's fine, Billy Ray. Surfing takes skill and guts."

Billy Ray checked his line, but there still wasn't anything happening. "You aren't going to try and talk me out of it?"

Milt baited his hook and cast it out into the river. "Why should I? Are you going to try and talk me out of the Marines?"

"No, of course not. That's different."

"How is it different, Billy Ray?" He pulled gently on the line but felt nothing.

Billy Ray wondered if it was just a trick question. He got that a lot in school and church. Adults were always testing kids.

"You're going to serve your country, Milt." He figured that was the correct as well as the best answer.

"And it's something I want to do," Milt said slowly. "I want to be a Marine. Once I knew that, I also knew it was nobody else's business. Do you get my drift?"

Billy Ray reeled in his line and put down his rod. "I don't think they're biting for me."

Milt reeled his in, too, and made sure he still had a worm on, then cast it out again. He studied Billy Ray's face. "Do you know what I'm saying, Billy Ray?"

"Yeah. Sure."

Milt frowned. "I don't believe you."

"Yes, I understand," Billy Ray said.

"You understand why I want to be a Marine?"

"No."

"That's okay, Billy Ray." He sat his rod across his lap. "I joined up because it's right for me. It's a life I can understand. I want to be part of something that counts. I can't let anyone tell me different on that. When it's all said and done, it's yourself you live with. It's yourself you have to please and satisfy. It's yourself that you answer to. Nobody else."

Billy Ray cupped his hands over his eyes to glance at the setting sun.

"Nobody?"

Milt sighed heavily. "When it's about which path to go down, nobody. You have to pick the one that feels right to you. Otherwise, you'll feel cheated somewhere along the line and regret it."

A strong breeze had come up abruptly as they watched a brown river otter slip into the water from the muddy far bank and paddle downstream, its rodent head like a submarine periscope, a silver wake trailing it. The otter swiveled its head once in their direction to look them over, but didn't break its smooth stroke.

"That boy sure can swim," Billy Ray said. "I guess he knows where he's going."

"Let's moon him," Milt said, and they did.

Milt could no longer moon otters or barges. Milt was a mass of decaying molecules in six feet of delta soil outside Helena, Arkansas, overlooking the Mississippi. He had remained true to himself and made his own choice without counsel, and it had been right for him, and fatal. Milt had always conceded to Billy Ray that even though he wasn't a churchgoer, he acknowledged it was God pulling the strings, and some strings were a hell of a lot shorter than others. After a few weeks of monstrously boring servitude inventorying plumbing supplies at Fleener and Son, Billy Ray became a one-man revolution. He intentionally mixed up the sizes of nuts and bolts. He stocked plungers in the curtain rods aisle. He pinned his nameplate upside down on his orange vest. He dreamed of lobbing grenades like Che Guevara into the Home Improvement Center. He showed up late and left as early as he could, and eventually his father gave up because his Rigid Republicanism could not understand rebellion or conceive of its root causes.

Fleener and Son staggered into a truce, an accord, an agreement, a treaty: Mr. Fleener was right and Billy Ray was wrong, but Mr. Fleener couldn't convince Billy Ray of that, and the conflict was apparently beyond diplomacy so hostilities were suspended, and they agreed to disagree and live together very uncomfortably and nervously while Mr. Fleener consulted heaven and earth and the Bible, too, to decide what should come next.

Billy Ray pledged to himself to resurrect The Plan and expand it, refine it, fuel it, shape it, and work at the summer job Mayor Sullivan provided him for saving Purdy Boy. He would save money, and when the time was right, he'd launch into an orbit that would escape Argus, and he would visit Milt's grave in Arkansas.

The Plan had wheels.

# 3

# Grace Under Pressure

Mrs. Fleener's exaggeration of his medical acumen and potential in bringing back Purdy Boy from the Wiener Dog Land of the Dead was so intense that she thought Billy Ray should plan for medical school. That and there was a palpable relief that Billy Ray had finally done something to imply he wasn't destined for a life of torpor punctuated by moments of actual malice.

Then she went back to baking cookies.

"Medical school?" Billy Ray said. "I'm just a sophomore in high school."

"That's not so," she said, sliding a sheet of cookies into the oven. "You're a junior now."

"Not till fall."

"You completed your sophomore year already, so now you're a junior. You have to plan ahead if you want to be a doctor."

"Who says I want to be a doctor?" But he had a sudden brilliant thought: Doctor Billy Ray, the Surfing Surgeon of California. It had a nice ring to it.

"What's wrong with being a doctor?" she said. "You could go to medical school in Chicago. It's not that far."

"Maybe I want to do something other than medical school."

She placed her hands on her hips, a pose that signaled a lecture on the way.

"Like what?" she said. "Surfing? Really, Billy Ray. Where does that come from? Doctors make a lot more money than surfers. Do surfers even make money at all?"

"They have tournaments," he said. "All over the world."

"Do they get paid for these tournaments?" She wiped her hands on her white apron. "Doctors don't have to go to tournaments to make a living, you know."

"I didn't know that," he said, and she shot her standard don't-get-cute-with-me-young-man look.

She peered through the tiny oven window at the cookies. "Well, you showed great presence of mind in saving Minnie Sullivan's dog. You know how she loves that funny little wiener dog. Great presence of mind is something doctors have to have in abundance."

"So they can rip people open and look inside at their guts?"

"That's what doctors do. It's a really important job."

Billy Ray sat down at the kitchen table. "I know, but I don't think I'm cut out for it."

"Why, Billy Ray? Don't underestimate what you did to save Minnie's dog. Grace under pressure is what Ernest Hemingway called it. Doctors have to have it. Did you know Hemingway's father was a doctor, Billy Ray?"

Mrs. Fleener had read all about Hemingway in *Reader's Digest* at the dentist.

"Yeah, I read about it in English class," he said. "He killed himself."

"I know that Ernest Hemingway killed himself." She poked the cookies with a butter knife to see if they were done. "It was just a few years ago."

"I meant his father," Billy Ray said.

She wiped her hands again on her apron. "What about his father?"

*Reader's Digest* had left that detail out.

"Hemingway's father killed himself, too," he said. "He was a doctor, but he killed himself. With a gun."

"I didn't know that," she said. "Here, try this cookie."

He took a bite. "Still too soft."

"I thought so," she said. "You know, not all doctors kill themselves. Probably not many at all. That's just one case. Is that why you can't be a doctor?"

"No." He looked away for a moment. "I can't be a doctor because when my health class went to ISU back in January, we visited a really creepy cadaver lab."

Her mouth hung open a little. "You didn't tell me that. How come you never mentioned it?"

"I don't know." Billy Ray looked off into space again.

She looked a little shocked. "I'm surprised you didn't tell me about it."

"What's there to tell, Mom? It was just part of our field trip. You signed the permission slip."

"I know, but it didn't say anything about you kids seeing something like that. I would have liked to know about it ahead of time."

"I guess they forgot to mention it on the slip," Billy Ray said. "Would you have still signed if you'd known about it?"

She rubbed her nose absently and seemed a little stunned. "I don't know. I really don't."

"Well, I'm sorry," he said. "It was a shock for me, too. When some of the guys mentioned it, I thought they were just kidding. And then we went and walked into this room, and there they were."

"Dead people," she said flatly.

Billy Ray blinked his eyes a few times. "Moss Newbury called them stiffs, and the attendant gave him a dirty look. One of them—one of the cadavers—was some old guy from Bloomington who'd donated his body to science. He looked like he was smiling, but I don't know what he had to smile about. I wasn't smiling, and I was the one who was alive."

The visit to the cadaver lab had come just six months after Milt had died. Billy Ray had lately concluded he must be harboring some feelings and questions about death inside himself ever since. Saving Purdy Boy had actually made him ponder death a little, but mostly just as a fleeting, abstract thought. Now he knew the questions he couldn't ask that day of Mr. Fields, his health class teacher, while they hovered somberly over cold metal tables and gawked at transparent human wrecks: What was it like when someone died? How much did it hurt? And did they rise, like Jesus, and go to a better place? Could they look down on their former bodies and marvel at what they had once been?

A marine at the memorial service for Milt in Argus had told him soldiers' deaths were nothing like on TV shows, such as *Combat*, where Vic Morrow would gun down Germans with his tommy gun and they'd just sort of plop over and look like they were sleeping. But the marine stopped short of gory details, and Billy Ray had been afraid to ask more. He had hoped for answers when he finally reached Arkansas and Milt's grave. He regretted not going to the funeral in Helena, but he had just had his tonsils out and was too sick to make the trip. When they had given him the ether to put him out for the operation, Billy Ray had floated a moment in the fuzzy no man's land between reality and unconscious and saw Milt beckoning to him with a smile and a sparkling halo circling his head.

Mrs. Fleener could see he was lost in thought. "Tell me more about it, Billy Ray."

He could picture the cadavers, and he remembered, too, the stale, gray odor of the room.

"There were all these men, and some women, too. They were all sectioned into layers. They were like human onions. You could see their veins and arteries and livers and hearts—everything."

He had a fleeting thought of Milt in sections, but managed to suppress it.

Mrs. Fleener put a hand to her mouth and talked through it. "How did you feel about what you saw?"

He squirmed in the chair. "I didn't feel like becoming a doctor, that's for sure."

"That's all? That's all you felt?"

He chewed his lower lip and avoided her eyes. "I didn't feel anything," he lied. "It was just creepy, that's all."

"Nothing, Billy Ray? Nothing?"

"No, nothing. I didn't feel anything."

"I see," she said. "Well, did it make you think of your Uncle Milt?"

He knew he couldn't dodge that one. "Yeah. I did think about Milt."

They sat quietly for a while, and then the cookies were finally done. They were chocolate chip. She poured them both glasses of milk. Her glass had Bugs Bunny on it and his had Daffy Duck. They munched their cookies in silence until one of the neighbors started a lawn mower, but the noise faded after awhile.

"Death is part of life, Billy Ray," she said.

He munched faster until his cookie was gone. He reached for another. He was trying not to think about death, or even ever getting sick. He didn't believe death was part of anything but death and should be avoided at all costs. If it really was part of life, it would be called something else—something better, nicer.

"Say something, Billy Ray."

He reached for a washcloth hanging over the back of a chair and wiped cookie crumbs off his hands and mouth.

"I remember a Hemingway story from English class last year," he said. "At the end, a boy a lot younger than me asks his dad if dying is easy."

She stared back at him quite a while in that quiet little kitchen, and all the while Billy Ray felt like he was in the hot glare of a spotlight.

"Oh, my goodness," she said. "You're asking me, aren't you." Her face was a little red.

Billy Ray thought again of Vic Morrow and Germans throwing up their hands or clutching their chests or arms or wherever it was Sgt. Saunders got them—usually in the gut— and then flopping around for a moment before The Big TV Sleep. On TV the soon-to-be-dead asked for water and then their mothers, and although it was just actors, Billy Ray had begun to suspect that what the marine had wanted to tell him at Milt's service was that death could be horrible and noisy and hurt more than anyone could imagine.

Mrs. Fleener started to speak, but the lawn mower grew very loud again for a minute before it gradually retreated.

"You know," he said, "Purdy Boy didn't seem to be suffering at all before he came back to life." He met his mother's gaze. "I don't know if he actually died and then came back or what, but he seemed peaceful right up until when he opened his eyes. He sure did look surprised, though."

"I'll bet he was," she said, fidgeting for a bit with her empty glass. She got up and rooted around in the utensils drawer for a while, but didn't take anything out. The baking sheet was in the sink and she fetched it, wiped it off carefully, and placed it on one of the counters.

"We ate all the cookies," she said. "I have to make another batch. Your father will want some."

"He doesn't like chocolate chip," Billy Ray said to her back.

"I know. I'll make oatmeal."

Billy Ray went to the refrigerator and filled his glass again with milk. He looked out the kitchen door and saw the Nelsons' cat next door. It was stalking something in the tall evergreen bushes.

Behind him his mother asked, "Billy Ray, are you really going to become a surfer?"

He turned back to her. She was busy making cookie shapes.

"I don't know," he said. "I just might."

# 4

# Same Old, Same Old

It was customary during the week for Mr. Fleener to go home for dinner at precisely 5 p.m. and then return to the hardware store for an hour to give the night crew their marching orders. It was twelve blocks and four stoplights from the house to the store, and Mr. Fleener invariably arrived home at 5:10, and rarely later than 5:12. Dinner was ready by 4:45, and Mrs. Fleener kept everything warm on the stove until Mr. Fleener made his entrance. Then she would make a ceremony out of transferring dishes to the table because Mr. Fleener once remarked that hearing the tinkling of dishes got his stomach acids ready for eating.

Billy Ray explained to his mother that he wanted to eat early because he'd promised to meet Moss Newbury a little after 5, and a promise was a promise—not to mention that the Fleener and Son Shaky Peace Treaty always worked best when the antagonists didn't see each other for fear of air strikes and artillery barrages, and so Billy Ray wolfed down his fried chicken—a thigh, a breast, and a leg—plus peas, cauliflower, and carrots from 4:45 to 5:05, then bolted out the back door and circled around the house before his father pulled into the driveway precisely at 5:10.

Billy Ray didn't really have an appointment to meet up with Moss Newbury, though he figured that if he went by Monical's Pizza he'd see Moss because that's where he worked Monday, Tuesday, and Wednesday nights from chopping pepperoni—beating his meat, he liked to call it—and delivering pizzas when drivers were late or didn't show up.

Billy Ray could just picture the lecture he knew his father wanted to give him but was too perplexed yet to articulate because he was still in the bewilderment stage of discovering his son was an ungrateful malcontent. But if he could deliver The Speech, it would be a really terse man-to-foolish-dissident on his concerns that Billy Ray might yet be doomed to hell in a hand basket if he didn't start embracing his responsibilities as a fool expected to somehow blossom into manhood and vote Republican.

And the Purdy Boy Affair in Technicolor was sure to awaken in Mr. Fleener, Billy Ray knew, a renewed sense that time was running out, that Billy Ray had been thrust into the cruel glare of life and its myriad possibilities for hardship, tragedy, and brutality if one didn't summon an enormous amount of energy and faith and channel it into being a good Republican who took care of whatever needed to be taken care of.

Billy Ray almost regretted that he had hauled Purdy Boy's raggy ass out of Cottage Pond—almost, because Billy Ray was by no means a callous or indifferent boy and would have rescued that wiener dog whether it had belonged to Minnie Sullivan or Adolf Hitler. Had someone else, say Moss Newbury—or the nubile Margie Heinrich—had the honor of fetching the pooch that day, then Mr. Fleener's head would still be spinning with dreams of crescent wrenches and lubricants and plumbing fixtures, and Billy Ray could have cruised along relatively unmolested down the path to hell in a hand bag.

He found Moss smoking a cigarette behind the Monical's building. Moss was an inch shorter than Billy Ray, but stockier and blonde.

"A ciggy break already, Moss? Didn't you just start at five?"

"Keep your voice down. Mr. Khatchaturian don't know I'm out here. He's counting money in his office."

"Be honest, Moss. Do you always wash your hands after you smoke a cig, or go to the pisser?"

"Always," Moss said. "Unless I'm making a pizza for you."

"That's why I don't eat here, man."

"Plenty do," Moss said.

"You going to wash after that one?"

"Fucking aye, man. Khatchaturian always grabs me after my breaks and points me to the head. We get fined a quarter if they know we didn't wash. Adds up."

"You said he didn't know you're out here."

"He's got eyes in the back of his head, Billy Ray. You don't fuck with that guy."

Moss took a last hit and flicked the butt into water still standing from the morning rain. He glanced at his watch. "Dinner time at the Fleener house. Are you avoiding your old man again?"

"Does a fat dog fart?"

"All the time. Your old man still bugging you about surfing and becoming a straight arrow?"

"For sure. He says I'll end up a bum if I don't straighten up and get my act together."

"You are a bum, Billy Ray. But do you think you really need to straighten up?"

Billy Ray shrugged. "I think I'm sixteen, going on seventeen. It's not like I'm an astronaut or something."

"So, how does it feel to be a local hero?"

Billy Ray looked at his penny loafers for a second. "I'd rather it made Margie Heinrich warm up to me. Maybe out at Cottage Pond."

Moss chuckled. "Not much chance of that, dickhead."

"Why not?" Billy Ray didn't understand why everybody thought Margie was so unattainable. Somebody had to get in her pants. He figured it should be him as much as anyone else. More, maybe. Hero's reward.

"Because I told her you have a small weenie," Moss said.

"You did what?"

"You heard me. She was in here last night with those bitch girlfriends. They don't tip worth a shit, by the way. I'm supposed to put two pieces of pepperoni on each slice, but when it's them, I just put on one."

"Nice guy," Billy Ray said. "Did you really tell her that?"

"Sure did. But she said she'd already figured that out."

"No way," Billy Ray said. He wondered whether a girl could tell about those things by just looking at his pants. "You didn't tell her that."

"Sure I did."

"You're lying." Billy Ray leaned against Khatchaturian's new red Camaro parked by the back door. He held his hands just an inch from the window glass. "I'll spit on the windshield, too," he said.

"Hey," Moss yelled. "Don't smudge those fucking windows. He's a maniac about that Camaro, man. The big hairy turd will can me if anything happens to it."

"I mean it," Billy Ray said.

Moss closed the back door and snuck a peek around the corner of the building toward the front.

"Okay, I didn't say anything to Margie about you or your weenie. What am I, a homo? No way."

"Was she really here last night."

"Who?"

"Elizabeth Taylor, you moron. Margie. Was Margie here last night for real?"

"Sure as shit. Now back away from that damn car, Billy Ray. I ain't kidding about Khatchaturian. He's nuts."

Billy Ray stepped away from the car. "You're not lying again, are you? She really was here?"

"I'll show you the booth she sat in, if you like," Moss said. "You can sniff the seat."

"You crack me up, Moss." But Billy Ray wondered whether her scent would still be there. He realized he didn't even know what her scent was, but he was sure it was really something. "No thanks. Anyway, I've got to move on."

"You just got here, Billy Ray. You don't want to sniff the booth?"

Billy Ray shook his head, but grinned. "I'm going home. Have to get up early and see Mayor Sullivan about a summer job."

"You should have said something," Moss said. "I could get you on here. Just say the word."

"The word is Margie."

"In your wet dreams, Billy Ray. You sure you don't want to stick around and have some pizza later? We get free slices."

"With only one piece of pepperoni?"

"Naw. I'll make them myself and load up on the pepperoni, Billy Ray. Some sausage, too."

"Thanks," Billy Ray said. "But by the time I get home my old man will be too tired to bother with me. I can sneak in. He'll be asleep in his easy chair. I'll catch up to you next time, man."

"Far out," Moss said.

"Don't take any wooden nickels," Billy Ray said as he turned and started down the alley back to McLean Avenue, the street he lived on.

"Okay, man," Moss said.

"Ciao, Moss."

"Yeah, ciao."

"Hey," Moss called. "You still set on that surfer thing?"

Billy Ray kept walking and didn't look back. "I don't know why people keep asking me that."

**5**

# Surf's Up

Saturday.

Downtown Argus under a warm orange sun.

Midwest girls at Walgreen's perfume counter.

Mr. Teters swept the sidewalk in front of his barber shop.

Mayor Sullivan picked his teeth at Bunnie's Tavern.

Moss Newbury skimped on pepperoni slices at Monical's.

Mrs. Carruthers shooed a cat from her garden.

Frank Palmer thought of ways to cheat on his taxes.

Eddie Venturi installed a muffler at Pete's Automotive.

Billy Franklin unloaded produce at the IGA grocery store.

Ada Foote sought directions at Tip's Food & Fuel.

Clerk Tim Rieger masturbated in the K-mart men's room.

Nancy Hardaway frosted a cake at Delbert's Bakery.

Billy Ray's mother folded towels in the laundry room.

Billy Ray's father found a crescent wrench for Mrs. Dobbs.

Billy Ray sat on a bench in front of Grant Park, tapping one foot to the Beach Boys blaring from his transistor radio, the other foot rolling back and forth a skateboard with a red stripe down the center that he painted himself. He gazed sleepily across the street in the direction of Roger Gilstrap's

Texaco station, but he saw only sandy, warm beaches and blue waves dotted with grinning surfers.

A red El Dorado convertible entered his line of vision and stopped smack in front of him at a red light. Behind the wheel was Margie Heinrich, blonde and tanned the color of honey, her breasts straining against a yellow tank top. Billy Ray cranked up "California Girls"

*. . .The mid-west farmers daughters really make you feel all right*

*And the Northern girls with the way they kiss*
*They keep their boyfriends warm at night . . .*

Margie winked and threw back her head. Her golden ponytail danced on bare freckled shoulders. She located the same station on her radio, and Main Street was alive with Beach Boys. The light turned green, but Margie hesitated. She looked Billy Ray over, ever so slowly, allowing a smile to form, then another wink, and then she gunned the big El Dorado down the street. Billy Ray eyed it for blocks before it turned onto Lake Argus Road.

He eased back into his bench, the sun warming his face. Billy Ray could smell salty breezes and feel the cool spray from the Santa Monica surf. He smelled coconut-scented suntan lotion oiling bronze bodies in bikinis.

Surf's Up.

# 6

# Water as Blue as Your Eyes

The Cushmaker was telling Billy Ray how he got his nickname.

"Billy Ray, in the Navy you had to have a plan. Otherwise, you worked too hard."

Billy Ray shrugged. "I don't get it," he said, thinking it was a good excuse to take a break. He was wondering if he should have taken Moss up on a job at Monical's instead of becoming the Cushmaker's assistant. Billy Ray and the Cushmaker worked for the McLean County road construction crew shoring up a crumbling seawall at one end of the causeway across Lake Argus. It was sweaty work, but Billy Ray reminded himself that the county paid much better than Monical's, and he was out in the sun, which was so bright off the water they had to cup hands over their eyes to make out the far shore, which really wasn't so far. The wind had come up a notch from breeze to pissant annoyance and kicked up rolling whitecaps.

"Well, Billy Ray, I was on a destroyer," the Cushmaker said. "The *Carl Vincent*. Fall of 1942. We had this pimple-faced ensign who dogged us pretty good on the work details."

"Sort of like how Mr. Furman does," Billy Ray said, thinking of the county construction foreman. He stuck his shovel into the ground and dabbed his sweaty face with the bottom of his t-shirt. He took a hearty drink from the water jug, belched, and wiped his mouth with the back of his hand.

"What was his name?" Billy Ray said.

"Who?"

"The ensign."

"That's not important," the Cushmaker said. "But it was Arthur R. Featherton, and he was from Syracuse, New York. How's that for memory?"

"That's pretty good, Cush. Seeing how that was more than twenty years ago."

"That's right. And I've had a beer or two since then."

All morning Cush had cut down pipe with an acetylene torch, and Billy Ray drove them part way into the shallow water along shore with a sledge hammer. It was hard work, but Billy Ray liked how it made the muscles of his arms stand out. The sun had tanned him bronze. He was sure it made him look older, more mature, like a surfer from California—like in pictures in *Surfer* magazine at Walgreen's. Another crew would come along behind Billy Ray and Cush with old railroad ties and drive the pipes down tight to hold the ties.

Billy Ray stuck his shovel into the ground again. "Time for a break, ain't it? It sure is hot."

"Now you're learning," Cush said.

Cush eased himself awkwardly to the ground and sat cross-legged. "Learned how to sit this way at sea." He slipped his hat off and wiped his head with a handkerchief. The hat was blue faded canvas, like the ones fishermen wore with lures and spinners hanging from them, except Cush's hat only had a Stag Beer emblem on it.

"You were telling me how you got your nickname," Billy Ray said.

"I was a machinist's mate, Billy Ray. I worked with metals and such. I had me a little pail of water, a piece of pipe, and my torch. Those were my tools of the trade."

Cush took a long swig from the water jug.

"Sounds boring," Billy Ray said, flexing his biceps to see if they had gotten bigger yet. "Didn't you get shot at?"

"Oh, sure, we got shot at." Cush scratched his bristly chin whiskers. "We almost joined the choir that went down in Iron Bottom Sound." He looked off across Lake Argus, remembering those days clearly for a moment.

"Iron Bottom Sound?" The name tickled Billy Ray. It was so exotic compared to the names of places in east central Illinois, such as Bloomington-Normal, Gibson City, or Saybrook. "Where's Iron Bottom Sound?"

"Guadalcanal. South Pacific."

Guadalcanal was another name that tickled Billy Ray. He'd heard that one someplace before. History class at school maybe. Or down at the VFW in Argus with Uncle Milt, who knew everything about World War II it seemed. Billy Ray knew Guadalcanal was one of those places that made grown ups get serious when it was mentioned.

"Must have been some kind of place," Billy Ray said, trying to imagine an iron bottom under the ocean. "Was it pretty rough there?"

"Yes, sir," Cush said. He closed his eyes and it all came back to him and he was young again. "Pretty rough alright. But beautiful. Gorgeous. The sunsets were like you see in the movies, and I never saw water so blue. Water as blue as your eyes, Billy Ray. At night the stars seemed no higher than the coconuts."

"I thought you were on a boat, Cush. Where'd the coconuts come from?"

"A ship, Billy Ray, not a boat. Submarines were called boats. I was on a tin can. Sometimes we got on the islands to look around, maybe drink some beer on the beach with the marines and army. We slept under the stars."

Billy Ray said. "How come they call it Iron Bottom Sound?"

Cush looked down at the ground. "Because of all the ships sunk down there, Billy Ray."

"Oh," Billy Ray said. He was imagining ships littering the ocean floor, but they didn't look real to him. They looked more like plastic models he could buy from K-mart in Bloomington, put together with glue, and submerge in the creek near his house. He had assembled the Bismarck and Tirpitz, huge German battleships that cost only a few bucks and a tube of glue. "I understand. I guess we lost plenty of ships there."

"Both sides," Cush said. "Both sides are well represented down there."

Billy Ray passed the water jug to Cush, who waved it off. Cush dug a cigarette from his shirt pocket and lit it. He exhaled slowly and closed his eyes. Gulls circled overhead and chattered noisily. A dozen sailboats with yellow sails hugged the far shore. It was the middle of the week and there wasn't much traffic on the lake. A big Evinrude tri-hull emerged through the opening under the causeway bridge and the pilot shoved the throttle forward all the way. Its bow rose for a second and then smacked back into the water with a loud thud. Billy Ray could hear several girls in bikinis screaming as the boat sprinted south toward the dam at the south end of the lake. Billy Ray watched it until it was a lonely speck on the horizon.

"You never finished the story," Billy Ray said. "How did you get your name?"

Cush flicked the cigarette butt into the water. He was back from the sorrow of the war and even managed to grin.

"Like I was saying, you had to have a plan. So, we'd station a lookout somewhere to watch for that pukey ensign."

"Arthur R. Featherton," Billy Ray said. "From New York."

"That's the guy," Cush said. "He liked to stroll around our detail every now and then to see if we were busy. The chief gave the work orders and officers would just strut around with their hands clasped behind their backs trying to look important."

"Like Mr. Furman, and my old man, "Billy Ray said. "My dad does that at his hardware store. Sometimes at home, too."

"Then we can make you an honorary machinist's mate," Cush said.

"Groovy," Billy Ray said. He knew that groovy was part of the surfer lingo out in California. "But I still don't know why you're called Cushmaker."

Cush chuckled. "They called me that because every time an officer nosed around to see if I was working, I'd heat up my length of pipe with the torch until it glowed red. Then I'd plunge it into the pail of water."

"What good did that do?"

"Plenty. The officer would nod his head and say, 'Carry on, men' as he strutted away. That's what good it did."

Billy Ray studied the spreading grin on Cush's face. "Yeah, but what's that got to do with being called Cushmaker?"

"Think about it, Billy Ray."

Billy Ray employed a full-court press of thought and was pondering it when the county work truck pulled up to take them back to town. They loaded up Cush's torch and the shovels and climbed into the truck bed. As they sped across the causeway the big Evinrude tri-hull had re-appeared and was slipping under the bridge as the truck went over it. Billy

Ray could see the bikini girls again. One of them seemed to notice him and waved, Billy Ray pumping an arm back in acknowledgement like he imagined some Blonde Surfer Boy God might do on a California beach.

Down the road a ways Billy Ray had to cup his hands close to Cush's ear to be heard over the wind: "Cuuussshhhh!!!"

# 7

# The Nation Looks to You

By the end of summer, Billy Ray and the Cushmaker had cut and pounded all the pipe they would ever want to cut and pound. Billy Ray was sure his biceps had grown into Surfer Boy Biceps. He kept flexing them in different poses as the Cushmaker nodded absently and packed up his acetylene torch. The county truck was due in ten minutes. They sat in the grass and Cushmaker smoked while Billy Ray explained all he knew about surfing, which wasn't so much and didn't take very long at all.

After a while the Cushmaker looked at his watch and was about to say the county truck was late when a motorcade of black limousines trailing a white dust cloud roared across the causeway with a state trooper's car in the lead blaring its siren. Billy Ray noted that it was as unlikely a thing as he ever expected to see on the Lake Argus causeway and Cushmaker agreed.

They stood up and watched as the limos lurched to a stop by the porta-potty the county had set out by the road for the work crews. Men in dark suits and sunglasses got out and formed a perimeter so another man could sprint to the porta-potty like his pants were on fire. The man was Lyndon Baines Johnson, 36th president of the United States, and he was answering an urgent call of nature while on his way to Air Force One in Bloomington after enthusiastically sampling homemade chili in Gibson City that had gone nuclear in his digestive tract.

A gaggle of Secret Service agents herded Billy Ray and the Cushmaker away from the porta-potty to a stand of maple trees and told them not to move a muscle, which amused Billy Ray, and he flexed his muscles without thinking, and Agent Rob sprang to Billy Ray's side like he had the moves of a vampire. Their faces nearly touching, he screamed, "Whatingoodchrist almightydoyoufuckingthinkyou'redoingboy?"

After that was settled, and Billy Ray learned how to imitate a statue, and Agent Rob had wiped the spittle off his trembling lips, Lyndon Johnson emerged from the porta-potty looking considerably relieved.

"Now that's what I'd call hazardous waste," Johnson said to an aide, who smiled thinly but looked like he had heard it before. Pointing toward Billy Ray and the Cushmaker, Johnson said, "Who the hell are these fellows over by the trees?"

Agent Rob materialized vampire-like again: "County construction workers, Mr. President. They're repairing a seawall. We checked it out. They're okay."

Johnson nodded and loosened his tie. "Well, shit, let's go see what kind of work these boys do. A seawall, you say?"

"Yes, sir," Agent Rob said. "You see, they cut pipe and then pound the pipe, and then—"

Johnson's eyes narrowed. "I know how to build a damn seawall, Agent Rob. That's why I'm president."

Johnson went over and looked at the seawall for maybe three seconds and had his picture taken with Billy Ray and the

Cushmaker. Billy Ray flexed his muscles for the president, who even squeezed one of his biceps for one of the photos.

"You're on your way to becoming Charles Atlas, Billy Ray," Johnson said. "What do you figure to do with your life, son?"

"Who's Charles Atlas?" Billy Ray said.

The Cushmaker nudged him and said, "Man, the president of the United States just asked you a question."

Billy Ray though a moment, shrugged. "I don't really know, sir. What would you suggest?"

Johnson was amused. "Well, how old are you, Billy Ray?"

"I'm sixteen, sir. Well, going on seventeen."

"And what do you like to do?"

He gave it some thought. "I'd like to try surfing, sir."

Billy Ray noticed the Cushmaker rolling his eyes. Johnson looked out at Lake Argus. "Not much of that around here, I guess. Right, Billy Ray?"

"No, sir. Not really. But you should see the waves on a really windy day. The whitecaps get to rolling pretty good. I've tried using a surf board behind a boat, like a giant slalom ski."

Johnson looked again at the lake, which was smooth as glass. "That pretty satisfactory, a surfboard behind a boat?"

"Not really," Billy Ray said. "I guess I'll have to go out to California. It's magical out there."

Johnson frowned. "There's nothing magical about California. It's got its problem like any other place. Maybe more."

"I meant the waves in California are magical," Billy Ray said. "I've never actually been there."

"Well, I've been there plenty of times, "Johnson said. "Going there next week, as a matter of fact. Say, son, are you a Democrat?"

Billy Ray wasn't sure what he was in the politics department. "My dad's a Republican. I don't know. I haven't thought about it much, I guess."

Johnson signaled his entourage it was time to go. "Well, Billy Ray, just remember this. Young people are our future. The nation looks to you, Billy Ray. Choose wisely."

Billy Ray said he'd do his best, and Johnson climbed back in his limo with Agent Rob. When the limo pulled out onto the road it threw loose gravel on Billy Ray's and the Cushmaker's work boots. Johnson waved, and Billy Ray waved back, though he was tempted to give the finger just to get a rise out of Agent Rob, but he remembered that Agent Rob had a gun, so he dropped the idea.

"Well, so much for getting warm and fuzzy with the public," the Cushmaker said. "I wouldn't vote for the guy even if he did serve in the navy." He turned toward the other end of the causeway and saw the county truck making its way slowly toward them. The first drops of rain began to fall.

"Well, Billy Ray, you've met the president of the United Damn States. Did you learn anything?"

Billy Ray brushed raindrops from his forehead. "I don't know if I did or not. It's hard to say." Like a lot of things, Billy Ray figured, it would come to him later, when he wasn't thinking about it.

"He seemed like a nice enough guy, though, Cush."

"Maybe so," the Cushmaker said. "But my daddy always used to say you could give a Texan an enema and bury him in a shoebox."

# 8

# Easy Come, Easy Go

Margie Heinrich lived in The Enclave, a pricey gaggle of fake mansions rising like grain silos on the prairie outside Argus. Her family owned the Chrysler dealership in town, dined often at the country club, and moored a teak-decked sloop at the marina on Lake Argus. A week before school was to start Moss Newbury picked up Billy Ray in his Corvair Monza to cruise around the lake until Billy Ray got up the nerve to head over to The Enclave. Billy Ray fidgeted about it for quite a spell, much to the amusement of Moss, but Billy Ray concluded that since he was a local hero and confidant to President Johnson, maybe the time was right to be bold and make his intentions known to Margie.

First, though, they hiked two miles up Statler Woods Road to the Sunoco on Route 9 with the deflated spare tire after a nail exploded the right rear tire, and the Corvair fishtailed half into a ditch. They were lucky the spare only needed air. Moss zapped the tire with the air hose and checked it with a tire pressure gauge he'd borrowed from the attendant, Jimmy Lewis, a boy from their school.

"I heard he got caught bopping his baloney in detention hall," Moss said. "Right there in the back of the room. He had the old python out in plain sight and everything.

"Slapping the salami," Billy Ray, said, getting into the swing of it.

"Wacking the wiener."

"Choking the chicken."

"Tapping the tube steak," Moss said. He zapped the tire some more and stuck the gauge back in. "Almost there."

Billy Ray leaned against a gas pump. "You believe that, about Jimmy Lewis?" He looked around the pump at the building to make sure Jimmy wasn't lurking. He could see Jimmy at the other pumps, the ones out front, giving a lady in an Oldsmobile change.

Moss zapped the tire again. "Why not? He's a weird fucker."

"I guess," Billy Ray said. He didn't know Jimmy well. They had gym together his sophomore year. He looked over at the other pumps again. Jimmy was tipping his Sunoco cap to the lady, and then she pulled out. Jimmy went back inside. There weren't any more customers. Jimmy was lean and angular, seemingly all legs. Billy Ray tried to shake off the sudden image of Jimmy sitting behind the register beating his meat when there weren't customers. Billy Ray felt funny for a second, noting that he often flogged his own wienerschnitzel, though invariably he did so in the privacy of the bathroom with a Playboy, or with his eyes closed and his mind fixated on Margie. Just where was the line between good clean fun by yourself and becoming a pervert? He made a mental note to steer clear of Jimmy if they wound up in classes together.

"Know what else?" Moss said. "Jimmy told me Margie Heinrich stops here for gas all the damn time. Sometimes she lets her dress ride up, and he can see her panties. What do you think of that shit? He says she does it on purpose. She knows he's looking."

Billy Ray let that image play a good long moment in vivid color. He wondered what colors her panties were. A girl like her, coming from a to-do family, she probably had dozens of panties, and those skimpy things called teddy bears—no, teddies, that left little to the old imagination. Lingerie like he saw in Playboy. Billy Ray wondered whether she wore red and black panties. He was certain she did. Billy Ray knew that red and black panties were signs a girl wanted sex. He'd read that somewhere in one of those raunchier skin mags, like *Galaxy*, he snuck peeks at down at Walgreen's when the clerks were busy.

"Makes sense," Billy Ray said, looking down and realizing Moss was staring at him. "She only lives four miles from here, and there ain't any other gas stations."

"Earth to Billy Ray," Moss said. "I meant about her panties, you moron. I'll bet that jerk off Jimmy really smacks the old frankfurter around after she leaves." He screwed the valve cap back on and rotated the tire around completely, listening for any leaks. "Okay. She's ready."

On the way back down Statler Woods Road they took turns rolling the tire, but Billy Ray lost control of it on Turner Hill, which really wasn't a hill so much as a steep incline that ran by an abandoned farmhouse, and the tire took on a life of its own. It picked up velocity and veered off the road at the base of the hill and hopped a spindly fence corralling Old Man Dunstall's Herefords. That tire really had gathered up some speed and looked to Moss like a tire flying out of control at stock car races at the McLean County Fair, or even the Indianapolis 500 on TV. Billy Ray thought it was more like a Civil War cannonball skipping along the ground the way a good flat stone would on the surface of Lake Argus. Either way, that tire was a gnarled old 15-inch Goodyear with a heavy steel rim, and it smacked broadside into the largest Hereford with enough force to poleaxe the cow into a mud bog, which caused several nearby Herefords to panic, lose their footing in the mud, and fall, too, which caught the attention of Old Man Dunstall, who heard his cows bleat like lost sheep.

Billy Ray and Moss thought about just melting away into the forest and making their way around the lake, the loss of the tire a valuable and costly lesson, but Old Man Dunstall was an amiable enough farmer who'd been young once himself, and he thought the sight of his Herefords mud wrestling was sort of comical after he got over the surprise of it. That and the fact that none of the cows were really hurt, and the tire looked pretty good, too.

"Damned if you boys didn't bowl my Herefords over like bowling pins," Old Man Dunstall said. He plucked a bar of chewing tobacco from his overalls and bit off a chunk.

"What do you have to say for yourselves?"

The Hereford that stopped the Goodyear was still bleating and snorting.

Billy Ray stepped forward. "We could hose them off for you, Mr. Dunstall." He didn't know if that would be payment enough for what they'd done.

"Call me Ebbing," Mr. Dunstall said. Now that we're in the middle of a mud bog we might as well be on a first name basis. But I ain't got a hose out here, boys."

Billy Ray looked around. The Dunstall farmhouse was a good quarter-mile away.

"I do have some buckets, though," Mr. Dunstall said. "Up at the house."

It took three trips from the farmhouse to the bog, each of them carrying two five-gallon buckets, but they finally got those Herefords looking as good as new, though the bog had grown materially with the addition of more water. Billy Ray and Moss were covered with mud. Their arm and shoulder muscles ached.

A providential rain erupted, and the boys luxuriated in it and let the mud ooze off them until they realized they'd carried those buckets for nothing.

"We go to all that trouble, and then it rains," Moss said. His hair had washed down into his eyes in uneven strands. He looked over at the Herefords, who returned the look with fisheye stares.

"Look at them. They're in hog heaven."

Billy Ray flexed his biceps. "Do these look bigger to you?"

"Bigger than what?" Moss said. "Bigger than two hours ago? It takes months with weights to get big muscles."

"I don't know, "Billy Ray said. "I think they look bigger. Don't forget, I swung a sledge hammer all summer."

"You must have clipped yourself in the head."

Mr. Dunstall drove his pickup down the lane and motioned the boys into the back.

"C'mon, boys, I'll take you to your car. It's the least I can do for all the work you did."

Billy Ray and Moss clambered into the bed of the truck. By the time Mr. Dunstall dropped them at their car, the rain had shut off as though a spigot had been suddenly closed. The sun peeked through charcoal clouds. Moss tightened the lug nuts down on the Goodyear while Billy Ray held it in position. They were so intent on the operation they didn't notice right away that a car had pulled up next to them. It was Margie Heinrich and her blazing red El Dorado. And Jimmy Lewis was sitting in the passenger seat. He tipped his Sunoco hat to Billy Ray, who gawked first at Margie and then Jimmy.

"Got that tire under control?" Jimmy Lewis asked.

Billy Ray couldn't speak. Margie wore Ray-bans, and her long blonde hair was covered by a purple scarf. Billy Ray thought she looked remarkably like Jayne Mansfield. He attempted to spruce up some and brushed back a shock of hair that had fallen across his eyes, but only managed to smudge his forehead with grease. She put her hand over her mouth to keep from laughing at the sight of him.

"Show her your weenie," Moss said, elbowing Billy Ray. Billy Ray shoved him back and flipped him the bird.

"I heard that, Moss Newbury," Margie said. "Watch your mouth, or I'll tell your boss at Monical's you give free pizza to certain girls."

"Yeah," Jimmy Lewis said. "You watch yourself, Moss."

"Why don't you just go beat your meat," Moss said.

"And deprive you of the honor?"

Moss lunged toward Jimmy, but Margie floored the accelerator, and the blazing red El Dorado fishtailed violently, showering Billy Ray and Moss with gravel and mud. They had to turn away to avoid the blast, but some good-sized pebbles bounced off their shoulders and backs. When they looked up, all they could see was smoke. They could hear the El Dorado's engine whine for a good long distance down the road.

"You okay?" Moss said.

"Yeah. One of those damn rocks just missed my head." Billy Ray brushed grass and mud from his face and body.

"Jesus Christ, Moss. I can't believe she's with that jagoff Jimmy Lewis. You said he was just a creepy meat beater."

"I know," Moss said. "Well, I guess he found someone to handle it."

Billy Ray felt hollow inside.

"Easy come, easy go, "Moss said as they drove into town.

# 9

# She Loves You Yeah, Yeah, Yeah

School began with the revelation that Margie Heinrich had departed for Lichtenstein as an exchange student. Billy Ray moped for weeks. Even turning seventeen didn't help. He forgot all about surfing and California. Seeing the smug look on Jimmy Lewis's face in the hallways didn't help at all. Billy Ray pondered wiping the smirk away with his fist, but Moss said it wasn't worth the hassle over someone as obviously lacking in taste as Margie Heinrich. And Billy Ray wasn't the brawling type. Still, the mist of disappointment threatened to become full-fledged fog engulfing Billy Ray, who felt himself slide the down slope toward . . . well, he wasn't exactly sure what he was sliding toward, just that he was sliding. Not even surfing could interest him anymore.

Against his father's wishes, and because other kids had them and it was apparently cool, he tapped into the money he'd saved from the summer and bought a pair of Beatle Boots for fifty dollars at Goldblatt's in Bloomington.

Black calf leather with Cuban heels and pointed toes.

Polished until he could see his reflection in them.

He sort of felt like John Lennon singing "She loves you yeah, yeah, yeah."

He felt—cool.

Mrs. Fleener was baffled that he tagged along that Saturday while she shopped for curtain rods. She decided it must mean he was growing up some and suspected nothing when he disappeared for twenty minutes to drift over to the men's department, make his purchase, and stash the boots under the spare tire well in the trunk of the Plymouth wagon.

The boots made him more than an inch taller and bestowed confidence, even a swagger. Of course he could never wear them at home, so every day after school he carefully wrapped them in an old beach towel and hid them on a little shelf above the garage door, behind some boxes. Each morning after his father drove off to work, he replaced the boots on the shelf with a battered pair of Thom McCann loafers—not cool at all—approved by his father.

He would sit and change on a splintered orange crate in a corner, out of sight from the kitchen window, which his mother often peered out while cleaning up after breakfast. When Billy Ray slipped a finger through the straps on the back and pulled the boots on, he enveloped himself in the sheen of glorious rebellion.

Sometimes when Billy Ray walked downtown and passed in front of a store window, he would admire the boots in the window's reflection. When he walked home he listened with pleasure as the boots thunked along the planks of the footbridge across Sycamore Creek. One day Billy Ray stopped in the middle of the bridge and looked down to make sure he had not picked up any mud. He kept a rag in a pocket to buff the boots when he got to school. He ran the rag over the boots a couple times as he listened to the creek below. Water rattled over white boulders and dropped into a small pool. The water was a black boil beneath the tiny waterfall. It was pretty decent fishing for smallmouths and bluegills. Turtles would shyly poke their snouts up like tiny periscopes from the shelter of an old maple that had crumbled into the pool.

After crossing the creek, he eased down a slope, careful to pick up his feet so as not to scuff the boots. A short walk beyond the creek was a deep ravine, but Billy Ray had been reading at school about the world outside his narrow existence and remembered that in California a ravine might be called an arroyo. He liked that word very much. Arroyo. It was so much more exotic than ravine. To twittering sparrows huddled on a power line above him he called out, "Arroyo," and then he announced himself, "Billy Ray Fleener."

Billy Ray sat on a tree stump and looked across a field at the house peeking through the trees. The screened windows were open, and he could smell his mother's supper cooking on the stove. He thought he saw her once, a face framed with blonde curls, flashing quickly in front of the living room window. He glanced at the sky and saw the red splotches had disappeared. The gray-cloud cover was drifting toward the horizon. It would be dark in a few minutes. Already the dancing shadows were at play all around him, but he waited until darkness had settled before starting across the field to his house.

It was a big Cape Cod, a farmhouse once, but the town had finally crawled out that way, and the cornfields were sold by Billy Ray's grandfather to make room for a subdivision. The old farmhouse was handed down to Billy Ray's father. Billy Ray liked the house and especially loved the winter nights when the embers in the fireplace glowed orange and blue, and the living room filled up with warmth and the light was low as burning logs popped and cracked.

Billy Ray eased carefully along a side yard to the back of the house and circled around behind the detached garage to avoid being seen through the kitchen window. He looked that way several times and saw his mother, her head down as she did something over the sink. By now his father had looked at his watch and noted it was about time Billy Ray was back from school. He knew that on Thursdays Billy Ray stayed after and shot baskets in the gym with Moss. What he didn't know was that as many times as not they'd skip shooting hoops to walk downtown and check out girls in Allen's Drugstore and drink cherry cokes. Time had reduced the Fleener Civil War to a simmer, but hostilities could erupt any time.

Billy Ray slipped into the garage through the side door. He kept a flashlight by the door so he wouldn't have to turn on the overhead lights. He reached up to the shelf where his loafers would be and at that moment he always felt a little anxious they would be missing and his father would suddenly appear, the loafers in hand, a scowl across his face, demanding an explanation. But his luck had held once more, and the loafers were still sheltered in the towel.

He slipped off his boots and quickly stepped into the loafers, looking quickly out the window on the garage door to make sure no one was there. He directed his flashlight at the boots. They looked clean, and just looking at them, even in the dim light, made him feel like he owned something that was him and not somebody else's idea of how he should be. He hated the deception, of course. It's not that Billy Ray was fundamentally dishonest. In truth, he was quite honest about most things—about the things he knew mattered, anyway. Character things. If he sometimes ditched playing basketball to ogle girls, well, he knew that was not one of the major things, and there was a little wiggle room to massage the truth.

He wished he had some stovepipe slacks like the Beatles wore—or those jackets, the ones that looked like army uniforms, the Fab Four wore in *Life* magazine—but he knew that was out of reach for now. His father would not approve of the boots, let alone his becoming a carbon copy of John Lennon, and especially not Mick Jagger of the renegade Rolling Stones.

The Beatle Boots, if discovered, could napalm the truce.

Billy Ray went to the window and looked toward the house. His mother was still at the window. She glanced once in his direction, and he ducked quickly. She did not see him, or at least didn't indicate she had. She was hard at work doing something, maybe cutting up vegetables for a salad. He looked at his watch and saw he had about ten minutes before his father would sternly glance at his watch again and officially desire his presence. Maybe even go out in the driveway, hands planted firmly on his hips in exaggerated frustration, and search for him as though he were an errant dog taking too long to find a place to lift his leg.

He leaned against the garage wall and stared out the window. His mother was no longer in the kitchen window. He thought, *yeah, sometimes I'm like a dog being let out to pee on a short leash.* Billy Ray was not an unhappy boy. Not at all. And he knew his parents loved him very much. His father was never unkind, just stern and decisive. He had a narrow view of the world. Billy Ray figured it had something to do with being what Uncle Milt had called "a self-righteous Republican."

Poor Milt. Billy Ray was not particularly religious. He struggled with Christianity. That is, he avoided church as often as he could, but wasn't willing to rule out the possibility of God, and so he prayed privately, sometimes thinking it wasn't a bad idea to keep an open line. Now he said a quick prayer for Milt's soul. When he was done he smiled suddenly, realizing that Milt would laugh and say, "Good for you, Billy Ray," if he knew the little deception played with the Beatle Boots.

Billy Ray exited the garage, his step a little awkward as he made the transition from John Lennon back to Thom McCann. He stopped in the backyard and looked up. The cloud cover had cleared and stars winked at him. The moon would soon be full. He found the North Star and some of the constellations he remembered. He knew how far away those stars and planets were, and yet they seemed close enough to pluck out of the sky. His father claimed Earth was the only place inhabited by humans because God had put us all here for a reason and made us his chosen people. Billy Ray wondered if that could be true. So many possibilities in that sky. Were there fathers with sons who had to hide their Beatle Boots, or whatever they would be called, on some world God had not yet revealed? He giggled and threw a crisp salute to the moon, which he figured was one of the potential sites for Milt to have set up shop.

It was past time to go in the house, but instead he went out the gate in the backyard and started up the slope of what passed for a ridge in central Illinois. At the top he marveled at the shimmering lights of Bloomington-Normal stretching as far as he could see to the west. He looked up again at the stars. Billy Ray felt they all converged on him, and he loved the feeling. After a while he looked down at his house and saw the outline of his father under the back porch light. He took a step toward the house, but the sharp bark of a coyote stopped him. For a long moment he peered beyond the ridge where a thick forest guarded the banks of the Sangamon River as it slipped quietly into town.

When it happened, it was subtle enough. One morning Billy Ray walked by the kitchen table, and there were his Beatle Boots, sitting on the kitchen table, the towel carefully placed under them to protect the table.

Man the trenches, he thought. War had erupted again.

Billy Ray wasn't even all that surprised. He remembered thinking his mother would be pissed if she knew they were on the table, even with a towel under them. And it was a smelly, dirty towel. "People have to eat off this table," she would say.

Attached to the boots was a note from his father. The tape was strong silver duct tape like his father sold at the hardware store for plumbers as well as do-it-themselves types. People his father referred to as sheep waiting to be fleeced. The note advised him to think hard about honesty, loyalty, and principles—the star-spangled Ozzie and Harriet concepts his father never got tired of proclaiming as though the government had made him the Argus Clean Living Warden for the 700 block of McLean Avenue.

The note directed Billy Ray to reflect on those important concepts during the day and report to the hardware store after school.

The note had been typed.

There was thought behind it.

Planning.

Purpose.

Billy Ray sat down and stared at the note and then the boots for a good five minutes.

Then he slipped off the McCann loafers and put on the boots and went to school.

In English class Mrs. Fieldstone droned on about Faulkner, but Billy Ray kept writing the same three words on a sheet of paper: honesty, loyalty, principles.

He wrote them horizontally for a while. Then vertically.

He filled several sheets.

For a while he looked out the window at the baseball field. A gym class was playing softball. Jimmy Lewis was one of the players. He hit a triple and raced around the bases, his long white legs churning up a dust cloud behind him.

With a bathroom pass, Moss walked by Billy Ray's classroom, stood just out of sight from Mrs. Fieldstone, and good-naturedly flipped Billy Ray the bird.

Billy Ray betrayed no emotion.


When he reached the hardware store, his father was in a surprisingly good mood after selling a big order of plumbing fixtures to a house builder. But he was adamant against the Beatle Boots and clearly peeved that Billy Ray had shown up wearing them. He steered Billy Ray to the back room so no customers could see them.

"They're vulgar," he said.

"Why?" Billy Ray said. He pivoted a foot and examined them. "Why?"

His father, a large man with fat palms and long fingers, crossed his arms across his chest and sucked his lower lip. He had a bristly crew cut, which made his large head seem even bigger, and wore a name tag on his white, button-down oxford shirt that said simply, manager.

"They look like something a n— pimp would wear in Chicago."

Mr. Fleener had never been to Chicago.

For a moment Billy Ray wondered what a white pimp would wear.

"Mom says we shouldn't call negroes that."

"Maybe so," Mr. Fleener said. "But they still look like something a pimp would wear—negro, n—, or white."

Billy Ray knew an argument was useless. His father was always right, and he regarded young people as inexperienced and usually wrong.

"I paid fifty bucks for them," Billy Ray said.

"They saw you coming."

"Lots of kids are wearing them."

"Lots of kids are wrong."

"The Beatles wear them."

"The Beatles are scruffy long hairs determined to undermine America's God-fearing society."

Billy Ray reminded himself that the Beatles really didn't have such long hair and invariably wore suits and ties, though he hadn't kept up with them lately.

A deal was struck: Billy Ray would donate the boots to Goodwill, if they would have them, and stick to Thom McCann loafers. His father would not necessarily forgive him for The Great Fleener and Son Civil War, but accept, like they did in Korea, a demilitarized zone and the illusion of a peaceful settlement.

Instead Billy Ray stashed the boots in the garage at Moss's house and told his father that he'd sold them to a kid at school, an alternative that his father actually found acceptable after pondering it a while. He was worried Billy Ray might be turning his back on capitalism and the American Way thanks to the Beatles, television, and Dick Clark's American Bandstand.

Satisfied he had somehow resolved everything and had set Billy Ray back on the path, however modestly, toward becoming again a civilized young man of promise, he welcomed his son back into the patriotic bosom of the family. He even broached the notion of returning to the hardware store on a limited basis as a deliveryman.

Billy Ray played along, but he didn't want anything to do with the hardware store. He knew that once he put on one of those yellow employee jackets with a nameplate, he would be come another of his father's slaves. He'd be back swimming among all the gross and boring things, such as measuring plastic pipe or memorizing socket wrench sizes. Eventually he'd be promoted from deliveryman to assistant manager, and then one day it would be Fleener and Son all over again. Then his dad would retire, and Billy Ray would be the guy everybody in Argus went to when they broke a hammer or needed a new toilet.

Outside, he leaned against the house and sighed. Something was approaching, Billy Ray sensed. He didn't know what it was. But he had the feeling something was creeping toward him. It was like those days when the Channel 3 weatherman warned that a storm was coming, but when you went to the window and looked out, the sun was shining and the sky was clear. He had a plan and he was sticking with it.

# December's Children

After Christmas, Billy Ray shaved his sideburns and decided to let his hair grow out like the Beatles, a revelation he felt was best kept from his father until it became obvious. He continued wearing the Beatle Boots, which now had taps nailed to the heels that clicked when he walked the school's marble floors. A week after installing the taps, principal Sparks passed a rule banning them and confiscated all he could find, including Billy Ray's.

A few days later, Billy Ray got suspended for a day after making a disaster out of a disaster drill.

"He led a group of students out to look for funnel clouds," Principal Sparks told Mrs. Fleener. "It definitely defeats the safety procedures."

Soon after that, Billy Ray impulsively flipped the bird to a husky senior from what he assumed was the safety of the hall outside Mr. Hillenmeyer's 8 a.m. chemistry lab.

"It caused Tommy Andrews to spill a beaker," Principal Sparks told Mrs. Fleener. "The resulting smoke cloud forced an evacuation of the building."

That netted Billy Ray a two-day suspension, and later that day Tommy Andrews caught up to him in the boy's locker room and punched him, requiring a cold compress applied by Coach Billings to stanch the flow from Billy Ray's bloody nose.

Mrs. Fleener kept the incidents from Mr. Fleener, hoping it would all blow over. One Friday morning Mr. Sparks announced an assembly over the intercom. It wasn't scheduled. Billy Ray just naturally assumed it must have something to do with him, but he couldn't think of any thing he'd done recently to warrant such special attention. No labs had blown up, and no food fights had erupted in the cafeteria. There was only the one minor incident earlier in the week. He'd snapped Sandra Stoller's bra strap right after English class. But that couldn't be it. Surely not. Sandra had smiled at him playfully, and everybody knew Sandra liked him—and that she was a "loose" girl who liked boys to snap her bra straps. Was he to be humiliated in front of everybody for that?

As Billy Ray and his classmates filed down to the gym, he heard a couple teachers agree it was probably another pep rally for the basketball team, which needed all the pep it could get. That reassured Billy Ray until he reached the gym. A fidgety Mr. Sparks waited with arms crossed on the stage. He was bathed in high intensity track lighting. He wiped his glasses very painstakingly with a handkerchief and frowned fiercely. The bright lights turned his bald head into a glowing dome.

Moss plopped down next to Billy and whispered that Mrs. Tuckerman's geography class couldn't locate Vietnam on the globe, and Mr. Sparks got pissed when he found out. Then he got scared the students were all morons with no futures and called an emergency assembly. Mr. Sparks had fought at Chosin Reservoir in Korea, and lost three fingers to frostbite, and was awfully proud of it.

Just the word Vietnam had an unusual ring that made students look at each other and squirm uneasily on the hard wooden bleachers. It wasn't the sort of word heard much in central Illinois, until it had recently become a daily hot topic on the TV news, and it came out of people's mouths as "Vitnam" or "Veeitname" until wise and steely old Walter Cronkite helped everyone establish a consensus pronunciation. It didn't sound like a country as much as a condition one could get from doing something wrong, like forgetting to take vitamins or not washing your underwear. To Billy Ray, Vietnam was not really a country but instead a dense jungle purgatory where it was something like 150 degrees every day and populated by little yellow people in straw hats.

To Moss he said, "Think Florida with yellow dwarves shooting at you."

But what really got Billy's attention that day was how Mr. Sparks managed to work into his speech that the Rolling Stones were vulgar devils who couldn't be trusted. It was toward the end, when Mr. Sparks had exhausted Vietnam and had switched to morality and "the new music." After the assembly Billy Ray asked Mr. Sparks why the Rolling Stones were untrustworthy, but Mr. Sparks was evasive and abrupt, just like his parents and most of the other teachers.

After school Billy Ray walked toward home and tried to understand what Mr. Sparks knew about the Rolling Stones that made them untrustworthy and how it was remotely connected to Vietnam. When he passed through downtown Argus, Billy Ray stopped at Field's, a department store near the little bridge across the Sangamon River. Inside the aromas of coffee and confectioneries mixed with the perfumes of many women enveloped Billy Ray. It was a pleasant substitute for school, which always seemed to smell sweaty. Field's was packed with shoppers, mostly women, but a few men, too, looking lost, discomfort on their faces as their wives rooted through the merchandise.

The record department was small and in back of the store, where the ceiling was lower. It was a bit of a forgotten area that mostly displayed classical music and Country and Western records. Billy Ray hated both, especially country music. All that wailing and whining about trucks and broken hearts and such. His mom tended toward show tunes albums at home, stuff like the sound track from "Hatari." She also liked jazz, which he thought was mostly made up bullshit, but sometimes it sounded okay to him.

The new music, as Mr. Sparks termed it, was still slow to gain acceptance in towns like Argus, even though it wasn't that far to Chicago. But Billy Ray didn't have to look very long to find Beatles' albums and some of the other well-known groups, like Herman's Hermits, Freddie and the Dreamers, The Byrds, Beach Boys, and Animals. And of course Elvis. Billy Ray had seen most of the Elvis movies. There were always lots of girls, and Elvis made out pretty good in all of them. But Billy had started to sense Elvis represented something he was beginning to outgrow.

He didn't really have a record collection. His aunt Gisele from Champaign, who still thought he was twelve and didn't see him very often, had offered several albums of marching tunes for his seventeenth birthday. He borrowed his mom's turntable to listen to them a few times when he was bored. He didn't really own anything cool, a concept that he was becoming much more aware of. In fact, his only non-birthday present album was Ferry Cross the Mersey by Gerry and the Pacemakers, which was a big hit and a ballad that didn't offend his parents. Billy Ray had bought it impulsively the day after hearing the title song, which some high school girls he overheard had proclaimed to be cool. It was catchy and all that, but after a while he realized he was looking for something with a little more bite to it musically, and the Pacemakers were sort of wimpy when you really got down to it.

The Pacemakers were nothing like the Rolling Stones with their outlandish clothes and hair wilder than the Beatles, and just about everybody else Billy knew about, which wasn't so much. His knowledge of rock and roll was pretty basic. He was learning as he went—as he heard other kids talk about it. But he knew, down in his gut, that rock and roll—not show tunes—was the way for him. The Stones were rebellious, even dangerous. They did what they wanted and told anyone who disagreed to kiss their asses.

He flipped through the racks and finally located the newest Stones album, *December's Children*. On the album cover the Stones seemed to be peeking into a door slightly ajar, except that Brian Jones, who Billy had recently learned was the group's leader, was sitting at the feet of the other Stones, his hand under his chin, a look of curiosity on his face, his blonde hair combed forward into what Billy Ray had to admit, until now, was strictly a girl's haircut. It was hard not to stare at Brian Jones. He was so odd. The other boy, the singer with the big lips—Mick Jagger—was barely in the picture. But it was Jones that Billy felt people looked at.

The only song from the album that Billy recognized was "Get Off My Cloud." Although he was still learning about cool, Billy was sure that "Get Off My Cloud" was definitely cool. He had heard it on WLS Radio in his parents' car, although they kept trying to get him to turn it down. Billy sometimes sang it under his breath when he was walking and sure nobody would hear him.

He looked hard at the picture of the Stones to figure out what would make them untrustworthy, but all he saw were five guys who had obviously hit the mother lode of cool. He bought the album, and as soon as he got outside the store, he took it out of the bag and walked with it face up under his arm. He wanted everybody to see that he was carrying a Stones album. He wanted everybody to see that he knew what cool was.

When a man and a woman about his parents' age briefly made eye contact with him on the sidewalk, he suddenly yelped, "Hey, hey, you, you, get offa my cloud" as he sprinted down the block. He came to an abrupt halt by a street light, which he circled once, his hand gripping the pole as he placed the other hand under his chin and posed momentarily like he was Brian Jones.

1967

# 11

# Therapy

It was well past the Fourth of July when Moss and Billy Ray shot off the last of their roman candles from Pruitt Hill. The hill shadowed a new subdivision squatting on the flat prairie. There were almost no trees except for a motley collection of saplings trucked in from a nursery. Each rocket hissed in a noisy arc toward the houses but fell short. A man came out of one of the houses and stared back at them, his hands planted on his hips.

"Some nimrod," Moss said.

"Yeah, some nimrod," Billy Ray agreed, though he wasn't sure what a nimrod was. The tall houses, so naked and stark, made Billy Ray think oddly and vaguely of grave markers in a cemetery of well-manicured lawns.

"Now that's really twisted," Moss said. He squinted and shaded his eyes with a hand for a sharper focus on the subdivision. "What makes you think of graves?"

Billy Ray shrugged. "I don't know. That's what came to me. You really think it's twisted?"

"Not really," Moss said. "Just odd."

"How odd?"

"Odd enough. But don't worry, I still think you're sane."

"Thanks," Billy Ray said. "I feel better already."

"But you might need some therapy," Moss said. "That's what my mom calls it when she goes to the shrink."

Billy Ray mulled that over. He wondered if his mother would ever see a shrink, but concluded his parents seemed happy enough, despite his father's strictness to conservative rules.

"Do you think she really needs therapy?"

Moss looked off at the houses a while. A breeze had come up, and Billy Ray thought the air smelled like rain, but there were no clouds to speak of.

"I think what she needs is to get out from under my old man," Moss said finally. "Instead, she gets therapy."

Neither spoke for a few minutes. The breeze had gained strength, scrubbing the branches of the oaks behind them. The branches rubbed against each other and sounded to Billy Ray a little like a human moaning.

"That's Margie Heinrich's house, right there," Billy Ray said. He pointed at it.

"I know, "Moss said. "But she's in Lichtenstein." He pointed west. "That's where she's at, about fifty-thousand miles or so."

Billy Ray looked west, but saw only a few cars and trucks and cornfields beyond. He wondered exactly where Lichtenstein was and what it was like. He had looked for it on the giant globe in the school library, but it eluded him.

"Do you think she misses Jimmy Lewis?"

"I think she's in Lichtenstein getting diddled by some Lichtensteiner boy," Moss said, a smirk spreading across his face. "Doggy style."

"You mean Lichtenstein style, "Billy Ray said. He slapped the back of Moss's head playfully. "You still have a sense of humor. I guess you don't need any therapy."

"Not even a little bit," Moss said. "Besides, there's therapy, and then there's therapy." He fumbled around in a pocket inside his jacket and produced a brown pint bottle of Old Crow. "Let's have a snort."

Billy Ray raised his eyebrows. He was a little shocked to see the whiskey. "Where did you get it?"

"It's one of my old man's. He keeps his stuff out in the garage. He doesn't think anybody knows that."

"He'll miss it," Billy Ray said.

"No he won't." Moss took a sip, coughed, and handed the bottle to Billy Ray. "He always has five or six pints out there. If one is missing, he'll just figure he drank it. That's how it goes for a drunk."

Billy Ray smelled the whiskey on the bottle's opening. He wasn't sure if he liked it or not. He sniffed it again.

"Don't sniff it," Moss said. "Just chug some down. Haven't you ever had booze before?"

"Sure I have," Billy Ray lied. "It's just that this isn't my regular brand, so I'm checking it out." He held the bottle up to the sun and pretended to analyze it. "Looks like good color, though."

Moss chuckled. "How would you know what color it should be?"

"Experience," Billy Ray said.

"Experience my ass, Billy Ray. I don't think you've ever had a drink before."

"Sure I have. I just don't advertise it."

Moss nodded. "Okay. Fair enough. So what's your brand, if it ain't Old Crow?"

Billy Ray couldn't think of any whiskey names, so he took a drink to buy time. The whiskey burned his throat, and he feared he would spit it up, but he got it down. He had swallowed several big gulps, like he remembered seeing Clint Eastwood and Eli Wallach do in *The Good, the Bad, and the Ugly* at the Argus Drive-in. When the whiskey reached his stomach, it was like a small explosion. Then he felt warm and a little woozy. He almost dropped the bottle when he handed it back to Moss, who was visibly impressed.

Moss took a big swig himself. "Damn, Billy Ray. You're a real drinking man."

"Told you I was. Here, give me another."

Billy Ray was careful not to drink as much as the first time, but he pretended to take another long pull. He was feeling the whiskey.

He exchanged a smirk with Moss, who said, "How many names do you know for pussy, Billy Ray?"

Billy Ray immediately had an image of soft blonde fur between Margie's legs. "Well, there's pussy," he said with a giggle. He wondered if he was drunk. He'd never been drunk.

"That one don't count," Moss said. "That's obvious."

"Cunt. Twat. Snatch," Billy Ray said, his vaginal vocabulary exhausted.

"Girls don't like the C-word," Moss said. "They'd rather be called a whore than a cunt. Doesn't seem much better to me, though."

"Do you really think they'd prefer whore?" Billy Ray said.

"No, I don't think they care for either one. It's just the C-word is worse for some reason."

"It has a nasty ring to it," Billy Ray said. "Girls sure are a mystery."

"For sure. I guess that's why they hate it." Moss handed the bottle to Billy Ray. "A snort for the C-word."

After another swig, Moss put the bottle away. "We have to go back to town soon, and you have to pretend to be sober."

"I'm fine," Billy Ray said, but he knew he was not. His head was spinning just a little. Not enough to make him dizzy, but just enough to make everything seem animated.

"We should have cut it with some water," Moss said. "I didn't think to bring any."

"It's better with water?"

"It doesn't bite as much with water," Moss said. "Hey, I thought you was a real drinker."

"I always drink it straight," Billy Ray said. "Like marines do. I didn't know about water."

Moss studied him. "You ain't never drank booze before. Admit it, Billy Ray."

Billy Ray smirked and bobbed his head a couple times. "Okay, so what if I haven't?"

"Don't get your panties in a bunch. It's okay if you ain't a big drinker. Look at where it got my old man."

Billy Ray had never seen Moss's father drunk. He'd only seen him when he coached them in Little League baseball and Boy Scouts. He seemed fine in those days. Normal.

"What does your dad do? I mean, to your mom."

"He hit her once. That's what."

"With his fist?"

"No, the back of his hand. He was careful not to mark her up. It was just the one time. After a while, he cried about it. They didn't think I knew about it, but I heard it all."

"When was this?" Billy Ray said.

"Last year." Moss chewed his lower lip. "Let's talk about something else."

"Sure. Like what?"

"You ever hear your old man and mom doing it?"

Billy Ray was mortified at the thought. He couldn't picture his father with a boner sticking it to his mother. His father who was so composed and proper and concerned with rules and such.

"Yeah. I've heard the bed squeaking from their bedroom."

Moss giggled. "Pretty gross, isn't it?"

"Very gross. Let's skip this topic."

"Okay," Moss nodded. "So, how about your uncle? How long has it been Billy Ray?

"More than a year." Billy Ray could see him still, looking happy and tan and healthy in his dress blues, a chest full of ribbons. Milt had always been the one Billy Ray could count on to escape from the strictness of his father. Milt was happy-go-lucky and didn't worry about anything.

"Why'd he join up?" Moss asked. "Did he want to go fight?"

Billy Ray had to think about that. He remembered all the things Milt had told him about duty and honor and belonging to something that was bigger than yourself. Milt believed in those things, but he told Billy Ray they weren't things a man ought to try and shove down the throats of other men. Live and let live, Milt said. What's right for one man isn't necessarily right for another.

"No," Billy Ray said. "I think he joined up because he wanted to see some of the world. I think Milt must have been pretty damn surprised when he got killed."

"I hear you," Moss said. He fumbled with a button on his jacket, then looked up sharply. "Do you think much about Vietnam?"

"I don't know." Billy Ray said after a pause. "I guess I should." But Billy Ray had actually thought very little of Vietnam. Even when Milt was killed, Vietnam was not a real place to him. Milt could have been killed in Nebraska in a car wreck, or shot accidentally by another marine in San Diego, and it would have been all the same to Billy Ray. Milt was dead, and it mattered little to Billy Ray how it happened, or where, so much as it happened before Billy Ray could ever tell Milt how much he meant to him. Milt had been refuge from his father. A respite from rules and dullness—therapy.

"Maybe it'll be over by the time they call us up," Moss said.

But Billy Ray wasn't listening. His head had cleared some from the Old Crow fog. He had dry mouth and wanted to take a nap. They drove back to Argus in silence, just the wind pouring through open windows and rattling pieces of loose notebook paper in the back seat of Moss's car.

He slept late the next day, Saturday, and wondered why no one made him get up early. He dressed and went downstairs and found his mother and father sitting quietly at the kitchen table. His mother looked confused and turned away to the window. His father motioned him out to the back porch, and there without any hesitation told him that Moss had shot his father with his father's new Beretta shotgun.

"Oh," was all that would come out of Billy Ray's mouth.

Someone from the sheriff's office was on the way to ask what Billy Ray knew about it.

His father crossed his arms over his chest. "Do you know anything about it?"

Billy Ray tried to picture Moss shooting his father, but it was impossible. He couldn't imagine it. He stared at his tennis shoes. He felt sick to his stomach.

His father squeezed his shoulder. "It's an awful thing."

Billy Ray looked up and could see his mother's face in the kitchen window. It looked as droopy sad as when Milt died. He suddenly realized how much he wished Milt was around to help him understand things. Finally he made eye contact with his father.

"Will they let Moss get some therapy?"

# 12

# Riptide

Argus was enveloped in an invisible fog.

Farm boys reeked of Lavoris at Steak 'n Shake.

Moss Newbury stared at a wall at the county jail.

Mayor Sullivan recalled school with Moss's father.

Minnie Sullivan hugged Purdy Boy on her front porch.

Moss's mother was silent since the shooting.

Sheriff Jon Gill pondered keeping Moss's father's shotgun.

Bill Ray's mom baked cookies for Billy Ray's father.

Billy Ray's dad held a shovel like the one for Moss's father.

Billy Ray sat alone on Pruitt Hill. It had only been a few weeks since he and Moss fired off the roman candles, but it felt like it was years ago. It almost seemed like something he read about or overheard. A false memory. Since then he had visited Moss in jail. Moss didn't even look quite the same. He looked older. There were lines on his forehead that Billy Ray had never noticed.

Moss's voice sounded tired and brittle, and he'd lost weight. Moss said the food wasn't very good—lots of baloney, hard cheese, and canned lima beans and corn—which didn't matter so much because he didn't have a good appetite. The hardest thing was getting through long days and nights with no one to talk to. And the noises: slamming doors, sudden screams and yells, and deputies barking orders. And the smells: unwashed bodies, farts, belches, and oily hair.

But he was looking forward to the trial and a chance to see people again.

Billy Ray went home that night and prayed harder than he ever had. He prayed for Moss, though he realized Moss was perhaps in Beyond Prayer Big Time Trouble, and prayer alone couldn't clean it up no matter how hard he tried. But he prayed anyway and consoled himself by remembering that Moss said everything would somehow turn out okay and that there was a reason for everything and that his life wasn't really over despite how it looked, which wasn't good, and Billy Ray somehow believed it.

Then he prayed that Milt would appear and tell him what his own life was supposed to be about. He was pretty sure he knew that Moss must have felt enough anger and desperation to kill his father, but what he couldn't fathom yet was how a person got to that point because nothing in his own life had ever been remotely that bad. It was as if there were two kinds of boys—ones who would never even contemplate shooting someone, and boys who could find the motivation to load a shotgun and pull the trigger. As much as he hated how his father had sometimes treated him, murder never crossed his mind. Just freedom.

Didn't Moss know there would be consequences? What about his mom? Or did Moss become crazy for a while and wasn't responsible? Billy Ray had heard people say that around town, that Moss was the real victim, a desperate boy merely trying to protect his mother and himself, too.

Billy Ray was stuck in neutral in a perpetual No Man's Land when it came to figuring death. There was the TV Fantasy Land of Vic Morrow Shooting Actors on TV and Moss murdering his own father. And Milt, a soldier, given the mission of killing other soldiers, men in different uniforms, marching to another ideology, but men nonetheless. Milt had a license to kill, like James Bond as 007? No, that was more fantasy. There was a word for this among surfers, a technical term for when things got shaky—riptide.

Billy Ray gave up on prayer, at least for the time being, and tried to visualize Milt. He closed his eyes and tried to see him as though he might appear in front of him, in marine uniform, brass buttons gleaming, medals rattling on his breast, his smile a crevice from ear to ear, But of course Milt did not appear, and Bill Ray stayed up most of the night searching for answers.

Around 4 a.m. he finally knew the time had come to hit the road.

# 13

# The Secret Relief Fund

Billy Ray sat on a hard wooden bench with a gym bag full of clothes in the Argus Greyhound Station. It was 6 a.m. on a Saturday. He had emptied his savings account the day before and bought a ticket to St. Louis and then on to Memphis and finally Helena, Arkansas. It was time to put The Plan into gear and reunite with Milt. He didn't really know anything much more than that, but he knew that much pretty resolutely.

Three nuns arrived and huddled on the bench across from him. A couple of young sailors in uniforms too big for them smoked cigarettes by a window and laughed about something. The benches filled up with people of all ages and sizes, and Billy Ray was excited to be going somewhere that didn't involve Fleener Hardware. Moss had told him that mostly homos and potential murderers frequented the bus station, but Billy Ray didn't think anyone looked at all like a murderer, or even a depraved weirdo who might whack off in the john and leave the mess on the sink. But Moss knew plenty about murder alright.

According to Moss, a woman had been murdered at the station. Billy Ray had never heard about it. Supposedly it happened in the 1950s, and the woman was shot by her husband as she stepped on a bus for Chicago to see another man. She died with one high-heeled foot still clinging to the first metal step of the bus, and the rest of her on the pavement. Moss claimed there was a photo of it in the newspaper archives, her legs askew and her white panties revealed. He said the outline of her vulva was clearly visible through her panties.

Billy Ray wasn't sure what the vulva was exactly, but just the sound of it drove home that it was pretty much in the Exalted Ballpark of Love that he very much had wanted to take a swing in with Margie Heinrich. He figured the vulva must be well beyond First Base or even Second Base. He was thinking Home Plate.

Billy Ray looked again at the nuns, who smiled as if on cue every time they made eye contact with him. Their heads were completely covered, and he couldn't tell what kind of hair they had. Were they bald under that headgear? Then the image of the dead woman floated back into his head, and he was embarrassed when he wondered what kind of panties nuns wore.

Did guys ever get boners over nuns? No way, he decided, though, Moss had admitted he felt one rising up when he saw the photo and the dead woman's panties. Not a complete one, mind you, Moss had cautioned, just some movement. "Panties is panties," he had said. That made Billy Ray uneasy. It was one thing to get a boner over the bra and panty ads in the Sears catalogue, or those bare-breasted native women in National Geographic, but not over a crotch shot from a dead woman. He concentrated hard to make the image go away and concluded he had spent too much time around Moss.

The swoosh of air brakes letting go outside the station signaled the bus had arrived. Soon a porter called everyone to board. But before the bus had lumbered twenty miles from Argus, an unexpected loneliness settled in on Billy Ray like fog. Then it began to rain, the drops drumming hard on the roof of the bus. He could smell exhaust fumes and cracked the window a bit to let in some air. Billy Ray felt a little like a sardine in a can, but after a while, just the thought of going someplace that was further from home than he'd ever been made him forget his anxiety.

Billy Ray hadn't been much of anywhere in his life. Twice to Indiana to see relatives. But that hardly counted because it wasn't that far to the state line on Highway 9, and the cousins lived just across it in Williamsport on the Wabash River. They never stayed more than a day when they went to the cousins' anyhow. And he only saw the Wabash once, a flash of brown from a moving car. When he was 14 he'd visited Chicago to see the Bears at Wrigley Field with Milt.

They'd gone up on the train from Bloomington-Normal. It was a fine sunny day in early October, and they crossed the Kankakee River, which was surprisingly wide to Billy Ray. Milt swigged bourbon from a flask he kept in a back pocket. He gave Billy Ray a sip but made him promise not to tell his dad. The train had lurched into Chicago past dozens of old warehouses, some of them splintered ruins. Union Station had swarmed with fascinating strangers. To Billy Ray it might as well have been the dark side of the moon, but he enjoyed it.

Now he would see St. Louis, another big town—home of the Cardinals, although Billy Ray was a Cubs man. He would see the Gateway Arch, just a year old. And the Mississippi River. The driver had said they would cross a high bridge over the Mississippi. He knew it was much wider than the Kankakee or the Wabash, and he couldn't wait to see the slow brown water and huge barges packed full of grain that could have come from Argus. He had read about Tom Sawyer and Huck Finn in English class. It would really be something. All that and still he was a long way from reaching exotic Arkansas, a southern state—a Reb state, with Confederate flags and moonshine whiskey. Where Milt and his father had been born and raised and mooned barges on the Mississippi. Billy Ray was going to see the world.

In Lincoln, a new driver came on duty, a young guy with his uniform pants tucked into shiny brown cowboy boots. He had long, thick sideburns down to his jaw and those reflective sunglasses highway patrolmen wore. Once he had horsed the big Greyhound back onto the highway south, the rain stopped, and he was quick to dial up the radio.

There were plenty of empty seats behind the driver—just a solitary marine asleep across the aisle with his head against the window, so Billy Ray moved up behind the driver and asked him what kind of music he liked. Billy Ray was hoping it wouldn't be country. The driver struck Billy Ray as a country guy.

"What's your name?" he asked Billy Ray.

"Billy Ray Fleener."

"Glad to know you, Billy Ray Fleener. I'm Ray Thompson. You like country music, Billy Ray Fleener?"

Billy Ray sighed and eased back in his seat. "It's okay, I guess."

"Bet you'd rather hear some of that rock and roll," the driver said. "Am I right about that, Billy Ray?"

"Yes, sir. I sure would."

"I thought so. You don't have to call me sir. Ray's fine." He twisted the dial and found WLS out of Chicago. "You a Beatles fan, Billy Ray?"

"Sure. Everybody likes the Beatles. Especially John Lennon." He looked down and admired his Beatle boots. "But I like the Rolling Stones, too."

"I saw them on Ed Sullivan," Ray said. "That Mick Jagger has got some lips like he's a black man."

"I know," Billy Ray said, wondering briefly—was Mick Jagger a black man? "What do you think of Brian Jones?"

"Which one is he?"

"The guy with long blonde hair," Billy Ray said. "Plays guitar."

Ray thought for a moment. "The one with the girl's haircut? Faggy looking fella with those bangs if you ask me. But plenty of guys are growing their hair like that nowadays. The girls are beginning to go crazy over it. It's the coming thing, Billy Ray, mark my words. Been thinking about growing my own a little longer and cashing in on the female action myself."

Ray found some Beatles on the radio. Paul McCartney's twangy bass notes propelled "Day Tripper" into Billy Ray, who mouthed as many of the words as he knew. But soon one of the nuns who had gotten on at Argus moved up and perched uneasily on the seat next to Billy Ray, who had never been that close to a nun. He wondered what nuns smelled like. The nun ignored Billy Ray, tapped the driver on the shoulder, and called him "young man" in a stern voice. He looked up into the mirror and seemed astonished to see a nun.

"Yes?" Ray said. "Is there a problem? Your seats okay?"

"Our seats are just fine, young man. Everything's okay except for that music."

"The Beatles?" Billy Ray said. When the nun glanced at him, Billy Ray noticed she had a nose like a turtle's beak. And facial hair. She was fierce-looking, Billy Ray thought.

"That's who I mean," she said. "I won't use their name because that wouldn't do. But we—by we, I mean myself and the two sisters traveling with me—would really be grateful if you wouldn't play their music."

Ray was stumped for a reply. He kept glancing at the nun in his mirror. Finally he said, "Is it that you don't want me to play music at all? Or is it just the Beatles you don't like?"

"Yeah," Billy Ray said, a little surprised to hear his own voice. "What have you got against the Beatles?"

The nun shot a frown at Billy Ray. "Are you Catholic, son?"

Billy Ray stared at his feet. "No, sister. I'm not."

"I didn't think so," she said. "As I was about to say, it's not a question of having something against them," She glanced again at Billy Ray who looked straight ahead. "But I will not tolerate what they said about our Lord Savior."

"Huh?" Ray said. "What's that about the Lord?"

"Well it's clear enough," the nun said. "They claim to be more popular than Jesus. It's an outrage. It's downright immoral, and I think we ought not to sanction their blasphemous views by listening to their music."

"They really said that?" Billy Ray asked, not sure just yet how he felt about it.

"They did indeed," she said. "Just the other day. And if their music is played on this bus, I can assure you, I'll write a letter to the bus company. And the archdiocese will be heard in this matter."

Ray didn't need to be told twice and quickly found a country station playing Hank Williams. The nun nodded her approval and went back to her seat. The marine across the aisle slid closer to Billy Ray.

"Don't underestimate no damn diocese," the marine said. "I'm Catholic myself. I know. Hell, I was awake but played possum until she was gone." He looked over his shoulder to make sure. "Them nuns are tougher than a DI."

"What's a D.I?" Bill Ray said.

"Drill instructor." He took out a flask and took a sip. Billy Ray wondered if all marines were issued a uniform, rifle, and then a flask of bourbon.

"My uncle was a marine," Billy Ray said.

"Say he was?" the marine said. "With who?"

"What do you mean?"

"His unit."

"Oh. The fifth marines."

The marine studied Billy Ray. "What's your name, pardner?"

"Billy Ray Fleener."

"I'm Cal Sweeney, from Opa-Locka, Florida."

They shook hands, and Billy Ray winced from the man's strong grip. He also noticed that Cal's uniform nameplate said Morrissey. "Glad to meet you," Billy Ray said. "But how come your name plate says Morrissey on it?"

Cal looked confused. He tilted the name plate up toward his face and regarded the upside-down letters for a moment. "I'll be damned. Well, you see what happened is a guy in my company, Dick Morrissey, lent me this shirt because I didn't have any clean ones. I plumb forgot to take one of my name plates off to replace his. I'm glad you pointed that out, Billy Ray, before I ran into an officer someplace who wanted to make a big deal about it."

"Do you have an extra name plate?"

Cal scratched the bridge of his nose. "I don't have one with me, no. I'll have to change into some civvies from my bag when I get to Springfield. So, Billy Ray, what's your uncle's name?"

"Milton Fleener."

"Where does he live?"

"Nowhere. He's dead."

"No," Cal said. "For a fact?"

"Last year," Billy Ray said, feeling a wave of sadness. "I'm headed to Helena, Arkansas, to see his grave. I never saw it yet."

"He was special to you, your Uncle Milton?"

"Yes, sir. He was my dad's younger brother. He was only twenty-seven. Milt liked to show up unexpected and do fun things, like go to ball games or pitch horseshoes out back of the VFW hall in Argus. He always took me along."

Cal nodded gravely. "And now you want to go pay your respects and all that."

"Yes, sir."

"You don't have to call me sir, Billy Ray. I'm just a corporal." He reached for his flask. "I'll drink one to your Uncle Milton. I reckon you're too young, or I'd offer you one."

"I'm seventeen," Billy Ray said.

"That's a good point, Billy Ray. That really is. You're old enough to fight for your country right now. That's a fact. But the driver might get the wrong idea—or those nuns back there—and toss us off the bus, so I better keep the booze to myself.

"Thanks anyway," Billy Ray said. "I don't really like whiskey too much. Beer's okay, though."

"This here's bourbon," Cal said. "There's kind of a difference. I wish we had us some beer, though. That would hit the spot. So, tell me where he got it."

"What?"

"Your Uncle Milton. Where did he get it?"

"In the—he stepped on a mine."

"Naw, I meant where in the Nam. Where was he killed?"

"The A-Shau Valley. You heard of it?"

"Yeah, I know it."

"You were there?"

He looked down slightly. "Well, I heard of it. Everybody in the crotch knows where everything is, of course.

"What's the crotch?"

"The corps. The crotch. That's what jarheads sometimes call it."

"The crotch," Bill Ray said. "Sounds pretty nasty alright."

"Yeah, you get the idea," Cal said.

"Jarheads," Billy Ray said. "Milt said that sometimes. But he said nobody was allowed to call him that except another marine."

"That's right," Cal said. "That's just between marines as it ain't a polite term. No, sir, not one fucking bit."

There was silence as Cal seemed to reflect on something. Billy Ray was ready to drop the talk about Milt for a while. It still hurt plenty to think about him dead, especially knowing he'd been blown up, and there wasn't much of him that was really buried down in Arkansas.

Instead he thought about how his folks would react when they read the note he left. His dad would be mad, and his mom would worry. He had tried to word it so they understood he wasn't running away from home, that he wasn't unhappy or hated them. He didn't hate anybody that he could think of. He would go back. He wanted to go back. But first he needed to get a look at the world beyond the borders of Argus. And he owed Milt this visit. He wished he'd told Milt how much he'd meant to him before it was too late. Now all that was left was to go and say it to a lump of dirt and a headstone, but Billy Ray felt he had to do it for both of them.

There was one other thing: Billy Ray sensed in a way he could not explain to anybody that maybe when he got down there something would happen, and he'd be different. He remembered that Davey Pritchard said a couple months after his grandfather died, he went out to Rose Garden Cemetery, outside Argus, and stood by his grave and said everything he could possibly think of to say to his grandfather, good and bad, and that when he was done he felt as light as a pheasant feather. Billy Ray didn't know for sure what that meant, but he was pretty sure it might be important:

Cal reached over and tugged at Billy Ray's shirtsleeve. "You okay, Billy Ray? You look like you were in a trance."

"Just thinking," Billy Ray said. He looked back at Cal, who had pulled his bag down from the overhead compartment.

"We'll be in Springfield soon," Cal said. "Maybe ten minutes. I have to get off there and see some people."

"Well, it was nice to meet you," Billy Ray said.

"Same here, my friend. Same here. Listen, I meant to mention something to you earlier. I was going to tell you about something when I heard you say your uncle was a marine, and then when you said he had been killed, well, I decided to think on it for a bit."

"Think on what, Cal?"

Cal looked over his shoulder quickly and then scooted a little closer to Billy Ray. He lowered his voice.

"I'm a patriotic marine, Billy Ray, and a proud American. Do you believe me?"

"Sure, I do. Why wouldn't I?"

"No reason not to, Billy Ray. I'm a patriot, and as a marine, I sort of technically represent the country. Like your Uncle Milton did. You were proud of him, am I right?"

"Yeah, I was. I mean, I still am."

"Of course you are," Cal said. "And you want to honor your uncle, right? That's why you're making this trip."

"Yeah, I guess so."

"I can help you, Billy Ray. I'm in a position to help you out. See, at first I thought you might be what we marines call a potential patriotic donor. Do you know what that means, Billy Ray?"

"I know what a donor is, if that's what you're asking." Billy Ray felt vaguely annoyed that Cal seemed to think he was just a boy.

"I know you do," Cal said. He looked around again. "I just thought maybe you had heard about this. See, we marines, when we're traveling on leave, like I am, are always on the alert for people we know want to do more than just put the stars and stripes out on a skinny little pole in front of their house."

Billy Ray nodded. "My folks have a flag at home, and my dad has a bigger one down at his hardware store."

Cal patted Billy Ray's knee. "See, that doesn't surprise me at all. You come from good American stock. No sir, I'm not surprised one bit. But here's where I was headed, Billy Ray. See, at first, before I knew what had happened to your uncle, I figured you might want to make the standard $25 donation to the marine magazine, which helps get the word out on the important job we do protecting the country."

"You're selling magazine subscriptions, Cal?" Billy Ray had a hard time visualizing Milt selling magazine subscriptions.

Cal smiled broadly and patted his knee again. "You are sharp, Billy Ray. I'll bet salesmen have a hard time getting one past you. No, I'm not selling subscriptions. I'm providing an opportunity, an association."

"That's good," Billy Ray said. "Because I'm not some sucker, you know."

"No, you're not. Anyone can see that in you. It's in the way you carry yourself."

"Really?" Billy Ray said. "How do I carry myself."

"Like a man, Billy Ray. Isn't that how you see yourself, as a man? You're seventeen. Old enough to join up. You're not a kid anymore. You're not a kid sneaking smokes and lighting cherry bombs with your friends."

"No," Billy Ray said dreamily, remembering the bathroom incident at school. "I'm not."

"So here's the deal," Cal said. "Here's what I had to think on. You're past being a donor, Billy Ray. Because your Uncle Milton paid what we refer to as the ultimate sacrifice, you qualify for an associate."

"What does that mean?"

Cal rubbed his hands together as though praying. He looked down at his shoes for a long moment.

"There's a thing called the secret marine relief fund," he said. "There's a magazine goes with it. A special one."

"How come I never heard of it?" Billy Ray said. "Milt never said anything about it."

"No, of course he didn't. He was a jarhead. Jarheads don't talk about it."

"Why not?"

"It's special. Sacred, sort of. It's not for just anybody to know about."

"Then what good is it?" Billy Ray said.

"Good point. That's a logical thing to say, Billy Ray, and I understand that. You really are growing up, my friend. That's such a shrewd analysis."

Billy Ray couldn't suppress a grin. "Like I said, I'm no sucker, Cal."

"And Billy Ray, I'd be a sucker if I thought so. Believe me. But ask yourself this. If anybody can do or see something, how special is it?"

Billy Ray pondered it a second. "Not very, I suppose."

"That's why the fund's magazine has to be so exclusive, to make it special. Why, do you know that it circulates only to officers and defense department muckety-mucks?"

"What are muckety-mucks?"

"Big shots."

"Oh. No one else?"

"Well, yeah—the president, Billy Ray."

"Johnson?"

Cal smacked his palms together. "That's right, Billy Ray. Lyndon

Damn Johnson reads it."

"I know him," Billy Ray said. "I mean, I met him when he came through Argus. I shook his hand."

"Say you did?" Cal nodded gravely. "Man, that's something, Billy Ray. I knew I was right to approach you about all this. So, here's my proposition. Do you want to honor Milton in the eyes of the president of the United States?"

Billy Ray didn't have to think. "Yes. Yes, I do. How? How does it work?"

"Any current marine can endorse it, and it's done."

"You'll do it for me, Cal?"

"Absolutely. All I have to do is forward your uncle's name and your name to the appropriate person at the appropriate address—I think you understand I can't reveal that person or address—and a three-by-four inch ad will go into the magazine saying you, Billy Ray Fleener of Argus, Illinois, sponsored a memorial ad for your uncle."

"And President Johnson reads it?" Billy Ray said.

"Old LBJ himself reads your name, and Uncle Milton's, and then he shakes his head and says by God we will win this war because men like Milton gave their lives, and nephews like Billy Ray Fleener know what that means."

"Jesus," Billy Ray said. "That's something."

"It sure is. And all we have to do is send the note, along with your fifty dollars, and it's done, Billy Ray. It will happen as soon as next month."

Billy Ray blinked a couple times. "Fifty dollars?"

"I mentioned that. I'm sure I did."

"Fifty dollars is a lot of money, Cal."

"I know it. You are right, Billy Ray. But look at it this way, if it was free, how special would it be? Think on that for a moment now. Country clubs aren't free. If they were, just anybody would be in them. And then, well, it's not so special. If just anybody could get his name in front of the president, then pretty damn quick nobody would be impressed, especially the president. See? It would mean Milton was just like any other person. But he's not, Billy Ray. He died for his country."

"I know, but—"

"He died for you, Billy Ray."

Billy Ray chewed on his lower lip. He had to watch his money, but could he actually quibble over the price of honoring Milt? Milt, who had died for him? No. It was the least he could do. He dug two twenties and a ten from his roll of bills and handed them to Cal, who shook his hand.

"It's an honor to know you, Billy Ray Fleener. And remember, the president will feel the same way."

Billy Ray felt it might be the best and most important fifty dollars he ever spent. He was still basking in the glory of his newfound patriotism when the bus pulled into the Springfield terminal, and Cal said good-bye and hopped off.

Billy Ray opened his window and stuck his head out. "I forgot to ask about a copy, Cal?"

"A copy?"

"Of the ad for Milt. How do I get a copy?"

Cal ran a hand through his bristly hair and glanced at the pavement. "Billy Ray, if they sent you a copy, it wouldn't be secret anymore. And if it wasn't secret, then it wouldn't be special—right?"

Billy Ray frowned slightly. "I guess so. But how do I know it appeared if I don't get a copy?"

"If you can't trust your government, Billy Ray, who can you trust?" Cal drew himself to attention and threw a crisp salute to Billy Ray. "The next time you see the president on TV, just remember this, Billy Ray Fleener—he knows your name."

Billy Ray returned the salute awkwardly and eased slowly back into his seat. Then to no one in particular he whispered, "LBJ will know my name."

# 14

# Snookered

Billy Ray's LBJ fantasy was ingloriously torpedoed just five minutes after the bus wheeled out of Springfield, and he introduced himself to Randall J. Bailey, a tall, reedy marine captain from Somerset, Iowa, working his way to Camp Pendleton in California.

"There's no such thing," Captain Bailey said. "I'm very sorry."

"Are you sure?" Billy Ray said. "Cal said only muckety-mucks know about it. Generals and such. You're a—"

"A captain. See the bars?" He put a finger on twin shiny bars on his collar. "There isn't any secret relief fund magazine."

Billy Ray wasn't ready to give up on LBJ just yet. "The thing is, it's secret. That's probably why you don't know about it. Maybe they don't pass it down to captains."

"I work for a general, Billy Ray. I see all his mail and know about all his correspondence. Sorry, but you got snookered."

"What's snookered?"

"He conned you out of fifty bucks."

"Oh." Billy Ray eased limply back into his seat and exhaled slowly. "Yeah, I guess he did. Shit."

He pulled his wad of bills out and counted them again as though the missing ones might still be there, the whole thing just a daydream. He wished he could track down that damn Cal Sweeney and throttle him. Really slug him good and get back his money. Maybe stuff a dollar bill in Cal's fat mouth and tell him it was a tip and see you later, brother.

He stewed on it for a few minutes and then punched the back of the seat in front of him, but only barked his knuckles a little. Besides, he knew Cal would just whip him. He was a marine, trained to kill. A man. Billy Ray had never even been in a fight. He was only trained to build a seawall. All that worked on him a while and then he realized he was getting hungry. He hadn't eaten since breakfast, except for a Snickers bar he'd found in his jacket. It was only an hour or so to St. Louis, and he planned to eat a big dinner there because there was a two-hour layover between buses. But he knew he should start pinching pennies some to make sure he had plenty of dough.

"Maybe I ought to join up," Billy Ray said, surprised to hear the words come out of his mouth. He looked over at the captain, who frowned slightly and put his novel back in his lap.

"Is that what you want to do, Billy Ray? Do you want to join the marines?"

Billy Ray rubbed his chin self-consciously. "With a parent's signature I can get in, right? Isn't that how it works?"

"A seventeen-year-old needs a parent to sign—yes, that's correct," the captain said. "But is it what you want?"

"Well, it was good enough for Uncle Milt."

"He's dead. I don't mean to be disrespectful. But you aren't Uncle Milt. And you don't need to join the marines to square his death, Billy Ray. Do you?"

"No, sir, I don't think I do," Billy Ray said, and he realized it was the truth.

The captain fumbled through his pockets for a cigarette and his lighter. He let his window down a crack and lit up, the smoke curling lazily across his face.

"Billy Ray, you want a cigarette? Do you smoke, son?"

"No, sir. I tried it a few times. But it didn't take, I guess. I always coughed too much."

"Good. Good for you. A bad little habit I picked it up in Nam. All through college you couldn't get me to smoke. Back then my body was a temple. Now look at me."

Billy Ray tried looking out the window a while. He tried to distract himself by counting barns, but it wasn't working.

"Why do you suppose he did it?" Billy Ray asked the captain, who had slipped back into his mystery novel.

"He's not a very good man," the captain said without looking up. "If I was his CO I'd throw his butt in the stockade."

"What's a CO?" Billy Ray asked.

"Commanding officer." The captain looked up for a second. "Listen, I'm sorry about your uncle. I meant to tell you that. I'm sure he was a fine man. Don't judge all marines by the one that conned you. But every barrel has some rotten ones, I suppose."

Bill Ray was still rubbing his tender knuckles. "Will he get tossed out of the marines if he's caught?"

"I suspect so," the captain said. "A dishonorable discharge. If he can be found. You realize he gave you a fake name. And that Morrissey nameplate may be fake, too. A little disguise he uses for conning people."

"Yeah, I know that," Billy Ray said, although he really didn't until the captain mentioned it. "I'm learning all kinds of stuff on this trip."

"He might not even be a marine," the captain said. "Maybe he just wears the uniform to score some money."

"He does that for a living?"

"Maybe. There's all kinds in this world, Billy Ray. You have to learn who you can trust and who you can't."

Billy Ray digested that for a moment. How the hell did one know the difference? What signs should he look for in a face? Were thin faces more trustworthy than a fat one? What about tall people versus short people? The captain was tall, perhaps six-four. What did that mean? Did it mean anything at all? Or maybe truth was to be found in the eyes. Cal's eyes were blue and seemed innocent enough to Billy Ray, but now he knew that maybe good and bad looked the same. The trick was to get under the surface and discover which was which. But how?

He now felt quite hurt that he had been cheated. The pain from it was palpable. He was sweaty and flashes of heat tumbled throughout his body. Billy Ray got up and looked back into the bus. A few people briefly made eye contact with him, but most just read their papers or books or dozed or looked out the window. Billy Ray wondered how many of them were dishonest. His gym teacher, Mr. Brand, once told the class that everybody has a story. Some you want to hear, and some you don't. Some you pay for, and some you don't. That's life.

Billy Ray took another look around the bus. An elderly woman smiled at him, but he refused to smile back, realizing it might just be a trick. All of the passengers might actually be hatching plots to defraud him and he searched faces to try and gauge which one was the most likely.

He turned to sit back down, but took one more quick glance over his shoulder just as the bus passed under an overpass. For the briefest moment, as the bus jumped from light to dark and back again, the passengers staring back at Billy Ray were skeletons with laughing skulls and rotating pinwheels for eyes, which glowed purple and orange like the coals of a campfire.

# 15

# Get Your Kicks on Route 66

Billy Ray counted his money. Losing the fifty to Conman Cal had cut into his traveling budget, which really wasn't a budget in any conventional or business way—more a semi-educated guess of how much he'd need to skedaddle Argus for Helena until he figured out Part Two of The Plan. He estimated he was probably okay on money, but part of him figured to cut costs. Billy Ray pondered cashing in the rest of his bus ticket and hitching.

He glanced around Mack's Ideal Diner, across the street from Union Station in St. Louis. He wondered who he could trust to hitch a ride with—who was a potential killer, and who was just a regular citizen pledging allegiance to the flag and paying taxes on time without complaint.

Clanging silverware punctuated the hum of diner conversation.

Frankie Reynolds of Belleville, Illinois, selected "Route 66" on the diner jukebox.

Waitress Carol Bertram nodded and wrote an order, but thought mostly of her sore feet.

Cleetus Ward of St. Louis chose meatloaf, but worried he should have gotten catfish.

Arcadia Monroe of Collinsville, Illinois, dumped two packets of sugar in her coffee.

Gladys Carrolton of St. Charles, Missouri, hissed at her three kids to be quiet and eat.

Billy Ray counted his money one more time before digging into his mashed potatoes.

Travis "Wino" Bartlett of Danville, California, watched Billy Ray put his wallet away.

Leaning out of his booth across from Billy Ray, Wino said "hello." Billy Ray was surprised and stared back with a mouth full of mashed potatoes. Two young women and another young man were sitting with Wino, who had long blonde hair and a peach fuzz beard. The two women smiled weakly. One raised her hand and offered a peace sign. The two women were thin and sleepy with straight long hair. The other man had Indian beads strung around his neck and over his tie-dyed t-shirt in a ragged necklace. His jet black hair was aflame with curls, and he'd cinched a red bandana across his forehead. They were, Billy Ray realized, the first hippies he had ever seen in person.

"They call me Wino," Wino said, offering a hand across the aisle.

Billy Ray stared and chewed his mashed potatoes.

"Wino, because I like wine—so, Wino," he said, the hand still there but a little shaky.

Billy Ray gulped the rest of his mashed potatoes. "I'm Billy Ray."

They shook hands and in an instant Wino slipped across the aisle and glided onto the seat opposite Billy Ray, who wondered what it meant. Folks back in Argus would never just plop down in a stranger's booth. And there was nobody in Argus named Wino that he knew of, though at the Legion or VFW there were geezers who people jokingly called winos.

Billy Ray looked over at the other three hippies across the aisle, and they smiled as if on cue.

"What can I do you for, Wino?" Billy Ray smirked and waited to see if it prompted a rise out of Wino, who ignored the faint Midwestern jocularity and bored right in.

"Got a proposition for you, man."

Billy Ray's face reddened, and he recalled Cal the Conman for a moment. Not again, he told himself.

"You don't look like a salesman, Wino." He glanced again at the other hippies, and they maintained their thin smiles. One of the girls winked at Billy Ray, and he was vaguely embarrassed.

"What kind of proposition? Are you selling magazines?" Billy Ray congratulated himself on sounding a little aggressive.

Wino chuckled and slapped the table mildly. "A good one, Billy Ray. Naw, man, I'm not selling magazines."

"That's good," Billy Ray said, surprised at how forceful and direct he sounded.

"Because I ain't nobody's fool."

"Easy, champ—it's not like that at all." He directed Billy Ray's gaze back to the other booth.

"That's Violette and Skyler, and the mean-looking dude is Chess, but he isn't really mean."

Chess smiled broadly and the women kept their perpetually weak smiles alive, waving at Billy Ray as though their hands weighed a lot and they needed to conserve strength.

Billy Ray didn't know which one was Violette and which was Skyler. There was something sort of familiar about them. They looked remarkably alike, though Billy Ray didn't think they were twins.

"We're a band," Wino said. "Well, we're becoming a band. Once we pick up our drummer in Memphis."

"Cool," Billy Ray said, noting it was perhaps the first time he had so easily used the word cool in a conversation. "But what's that got to do with me, Wino." He tried his best to put some edge on Wino's name by raising his voice.

"Nothing. I admit the band has nothing to do with you. But you're a music fan—am I right about that Billy Ray? I saw you tapping your feet to Route 66 on the juker. Didn't I see that, Billy Ray?"

"I guess I was." Billy Ray had a weak notion of his privacy being violated. "But it was the Rolling Stones. It's from their new album."

"*December's Children*," Wino said. "I know. It's a cool album. We're going to cover some songs."

"Get Off My Cloud? Are you going to do Get Off My Cloud? I like that one real well."

"Sure we will, Billy Ray. I'm already learning the chords—I'm the lead guitarist."

"Really?" Billy Ray had never met a real musician, noting that the organ player at the Argus Presbyterian Church really didn't count. "Cool. So, what's the name of your band?"

Wino exchanged looks with his band-mates. "Billy Ray's asking the band's name."

The near-twins waved pathetically. Chess chewed his lip a second, and then his face brightened. "Hey, man—maybe you could help with that one. We don't have a name yet."

Chess slid next to Wino, and Billy Ray contemplated a pair of hippies up close for the first time.

"Don't pay attention to the girls," Wino said. "They did a fat doobie before we came in, and so they're wasted."

"A doobie?" Billy Ray said. "What's a doobie?"

Chess lightly punched Wino's arm and they giggled.

"A doobie, Billy Ray," Wino said. "You know. A joint. Those two babes are blasted. Wasted. Get it?"

"A joint?" Billy Ray frowned and wondered whether joint and doobie were musical terms.

Chess leaned across the table.

"Where are you from, Billy Ray, that they don't have joints?"

"I'm from Argus. Argus, Illinois. It's near Bloomington."

"They're high, Billy Ray," Wino said, shaking his head in amazement. "They smoked marijuana. Does that take you where you need to be?"

"Oh. Marijuana. I get it." Billy Ray remembered health class, and Mr. Brand warning that marijuana was the devil's tool and would make you go insane eventually. He knew that Moss had claimed he tried it once. Was that the reason he shot his father? There had to be more to it than that, he figured.

"Chess, I think Billy Ray here must be the last innocent soul in America."

"Could be, man. Very well could be. Far out, man."

Billy Ray bristled. "What makes you think I'm so innocent? I've been around. Just what do you guys want, anyway?"

He squared himself and stared fiercely at Wino.

"Hey, everything's groovy," Wino said. "Don't go Republican on us."

"Yeah, man—it's cool," Chess said.

"It's like this," Wino said. He clasped his hands. "You looked like a cool dude, Billy Ray. We could tell that right off because you seemed to groove to the music. So, we thought you'd be the kind of guy interested in helping a band get going. A band that's going to make a name for itself. A band that just needs a little nudge."

"You don't even have a name—or a drummer, yet—and you're hitting me up for money?" Billy Ray felt a little sick to his stomach.

"We have a drummer," Wino said. "We just have to swing by Memphis to get him. The name's no big deal, Billy Ray. That doesn't stop a band from being a band. Not at all. Look at the Beatles. They had several names before they got it right."

"Why do you need money if you're so good?" Billy Ray pushed his plate away, signaling he was ready to leave. He was sorry he'd ever left Argus if all there was to the world were con men and would-be musicians. He made a note to look at himself in the diner restroom to see if somehow he had sucker written all over his face.

"We're just running a little low until we get to Memphis, "Chess said, his tone apologetic. "Bobby Joe—our drummer— has some money to get us to New Orleans. That's where we're headed. He knows people there and can get us some gigs."

"That's right, Billy Ray." Wino sank back in the booth and sighed. "We just need a little gas money. We figured you were headed south, too, and we could hook up with you later and pay you back. Honest, we're good for it."

"We can get you in free to our gigs," Chess offered lamely. "Have you ever seen New Orleans? Man, that's a swinging town, Billy Ray, if you know what I mean."

Though he realized he was far from an expert on such things, Billy Ray sensed in his gut that Wino and Chess were telling the truth. But he was learning: did they really expect to see Billy Ray again and pay him back? No, of course not. He had seen Milt buy beers for men at the VFW in Argus. Weak men who all claimed they would pay him back. Now Billy Ray realized it was all fake promises made by men of varying degrees of desperation and addiction.

Wino and Chess were a little desperate, too. But Milt had once told him it didn't matter when he didn't get paid back because some people just didn't have the power to overcome their demons. You had to try and understand them and not just condemn them. The hard part, Billy Ray suddenly understood, was in knowing when to understand and when to condemn. He was learning that on the job.

"Where are you headed, Bill Ray?" Wino said.

"Helena, Arkansas. It's south of Memphis on the Mississippi."

"You have a bus ticket, right?" Chess looked hopeful.

"Maybe I do and maybe I don't," Billy Ray said. It occurred to him that life on the road was a lot like playing poker.

"Cash it in and go with us, Billy Ray. Help us with the gas, and we'll drop you in Helena. It's on the way to New Orleans. You'll save money."

"And maybe see Elvis, Billy Ray," Wino said. "We're going to go see Graceland when we get to Memphis. What do you think of that shit?"

"Elvis lives in Memphis?"

"Sure does. His house is called Graceland. Billy Ray, don't you know anything?"

Billy Ray locked his hands behind his head. For once since leaving Argus he felt he had the upper hand. And Elvis—that was a plus, too.

"Well, guys, I know this much," Billy Ray said. "I seem to be the key to getting to Graceland. Isn't that so?

"It is," Wino said solemnly. "The future of the band is in your hands."

"Groovy. Then in that case maybe it's time I got a little respect."

# 16

# Gravy Is Groovy

Leverage was a new concept to Billy Ray, but to his surprise, he instinctively knew how to wield it. After kicking in fifty dollars to the band's gas budget, he insisted on proof that Wino could play his guitar. Satisfied with what sounded indeed like the Rolling Stones, Billy Ray installed himself in the back of the Volkswagen mini-bus next to the dozing nearly-twins and also demanded a vote in naming the band.

"What are you, our manager?" Wino said.

"Until I get my fifty bucks back, I guess I am. As your manager, I'd say you need a name. By the way, who sings?"

"The girls."

"When they're not passed out from a doobie, you mean?"

"Yeah, something like that. But they look like Cher. Don't you think they look like Cher?"

"I suppose." Billy Ray looked over his shoulder at the comatose nearly-twins.

"They don't sing really all that well," Wino said, "but they're a visual thing. You need a gimmick to stand out, Billy Ray. "

"Do they ever speak?" Billy Ray said.

"Oh, sure. They'll talk your arm off. They just need to straighten up some. By the time we get to Graceland they should be in gear."

"I see," Billy Ray said skeptically. "Has this band actually ever played?"

Wino thought that over a moment. "We played a few bar gigs in California. Chess plays bass. We had a drummer out there, but he got drafted."

"Did you get paid for those gigs?"

"We got free beer."

"That's a start," Billy Ray said.

"Not really. It was Blatz beer."

"What's Blatz?"

"The worst beer ever. Except maybe for Falstaff or Stag."

Billy Ray recalled that the Cushmaker drank Stag at the VFW and swore by it. "I see. I'm serious about the name. It's as if you don't exist without a name."

Wino put the van in gear and soon they were rolling south on the highway through the flat boot-heel country of Missouri. "We have an idea for a name," Wino said after a few miles. "Gravy is Groovy."

Billy Ray nodded. "Yeah, I like gravy, too. What they put on my mashed potatoes back at that diner was a little thin, but not too bad."

Wino glanced at Billy Ray with a frown that evolved tediously into a smile. "Good one, Billy Ray. No, that's the name we've sort of been considering."

"Really? Gravy is Groovy?"

"Gimmicks, Billy Ray. Like I said, the music business is the gimmick business. You have to stand out. That's why we have two Cher look-alikes."

"Even if they can't sing?"

"It's not that they can't sing. They can. They just don't stand out as singers. But as Cher look-alikes, they stand out."

"Gravy is Groovy stands out alright," Billy Ray said. "Maybe too much. Don't you worry people will try too hard to understand what it means?"

"It doesn't mean anything." Wino smirks. "Chess thought it up when we were stoned. Somewhere in Nebraska, I think. Anyway, look at the groups around today. You've got your Moby Grape, your Jefferson Airplane, your Buffalo Springfield. Those names stand out."

Billy Ray had never heard of Moby Grape or Jefferson Airplane or Buffalo Springfield. And soon his thoughts had drifted back to Argus, back to Moss. There wasn't anything he could do about that. He didn't understand it and there wasn't anything to do about it. Casualties, Milt had said. Life piles up casualties. Part of the deal. You move on as best you can and avoid becoming a casualty yourself. But Billy Ray understood it was still new to him, and so he still was hurting inside for Moss, but accepted it was out of his hands. Life, that great maker of rules and decider of consequences, would sort it out.

Or so Billy Ray figured. He'd said his goodbye to Moss and even prayed for him. Moss was the only one Billy Ray had told other than his parents about hitting the road to see the world beyond Argus. Moss seemed relieved to talk about something other than his own problems. He understood that Billy Ray needed to escape, joking that he'd like to escape, too.

When Wino pulled over for burgers in Cape Girardeau, the nearly-twins ate lustily, said hello to Billy Ray, and then crawled back into their comas.

South of Cape Girardeau the lonely flat fields reminded him of Argus. He knew the Mississippi lurked somewhere behind a distant tree line. He wondered if he could smell the river and decided he could not. They really were in the South now, or what Billy Ray perceived as the South, even though it was just southern Missouri. But he thought it was the South nonetheless and even imagined he saw evidence of it on the faces of people he saw as they drove slowly through small towns and past gaggles of houses at crossroads. They seemed different. They looked different, though, Billy Ray couldn't put his finger on just what made them different. He knew that people referred to Southerners as rednecks, but there were rednecks back in Argus, too.

At a stop sign in Hayti, a negro boy of perhaps 12, Billy Ray estimated, shot a pea at him through the open window with a straw. It just missed him. The boy was very black and wore only ragged shorts. He was shoeless, and Billy Ray was struck by how big the boy's feet seemed. They made him think of Daffy Duck from TV cartoons. Billy Ray had never really met a negro. Once a negro family stopped for gas in Argus at Roger Gilstrap's Texaco station while Billy Ray was pumping up a bike tire. They were nicely dressed. The father gray-haired and dignified in a skimmer hat and gray suit. The whole family seemed to Billy Ray to be dressed for church or even a wedding or a funeral. They got gas and didn't linger. They had New York license plates, Billy Ray remembered, and everyone at the gas station glanced uneasily at them as though Martians had landed. He made eye contact with the father and said hello. The father smiled slowly, warily, and replied, "Young man."

That night at the Argus VFW Billy Ray had sipped a cherry Coke and asked Milt about negroes.

"Are there a lot of them in the marines?"

"Sure there are. Plenty."

"What are they like?"

"They're like everyone else, only different, too."

"Do you like them?"

"We rely on each other, Billy Ray. We're not black or white, or purple or green. We're marines."

Now it seemed like decades since that conversation. Milt was long dead and Billy Ray was finally closing in on Helena and Milt's grave to say a proper goodbye. That thought stayed with him a good long time, even when Wino sometimes interrupted his daydreams to make conversation about music, but after a while Milt's ghost dissolved and Billy Ray wondered what his parents were doing. His Mom would have called ahead to the cousins in Helena. She would worry about him but have faith that he knew what he was doing. His father wouldn't understand it at all and resent it, too. He'd give Billy Ray's mom the lecture he desperately wanted to give Billy Ray.

When they crossed into Arkansas, Wino said, "We're really in the heart of delta country now. It's not that far to Memphis. Can you feel it, Billy Ray?"

Billy Ray sniffed the air and looked over at the tree line. He really thought he could smell the river.

# Graceland

Wino horsed the mini-bus across the Mississippi into Memphis low on gas but directly to Graceland on fumes. Even the Cher lookalikes were awake, anticipating the first look into ElvisWorld. Wino gushed that he might piss his pants he was so excited, and Chess joked that he already had. Ever so in unison, the nearly-twins bobbed their Cher heads approvingly.

Gravy is Groovy had reached its Mecca.

Not so for Billy Ray. He was a little disappointed. Graceland clung to a modest rise, and although the estate's gates festooned with musical notes were cool—Billy Ray knew you didn't see that every day—he thought the house itself was somehow unremarkable. He felt it was sort of dense and squat, and he'd seen more pillars at the courthouse in Argus. Graceland was a bunker compared to Argus Victorians that towered handsomely like many-masted tall ships he had seen in history books. Billy Ray just didn't automatically picture Elvis Presley living in Graceland. It just didn't seem big enough or grand enough to contain The King. Or maybe he was just being contrary. He wasn't sure. Billy Ray was anxious to press on to Helena.

Perhaps overcome somewhat by the culmination of their pilgrimage, the nearly twins adjourned back to the mini-bus to smoke a doobie and meditate on the impact of reaching the Elvis Vortex.

Chess journeyed off in search of a store and returned with a Styrofoam cooler of ice sheltering a six-pack of Dixie beer, which he distributed to Wino and Billy Ray.

"Brewed in New Orleans," Chess added.

Wino decided they should camp out across from Graceland a while to see if Elvis made an appearance.

Billy Ray examined the cold beer in his hand. "I'm underage, guys. At least in Illinois."

"How old are you, Billy Ray?" Wino asked.

"Seventeen."

"Close enough," Wino said. "You're old enough to drink a beer."

"Damn right," Chess said. "You're almost old enough to go to Vietnam, and so you're old enough to drink beer. Besides, I think the drinking age is lower down here in Tennessee."

"That's probably true," Wino said. He hoisted his can of Dixie in salute. "Everything is different in the south."

"Salute," Billy Ray said. He downed a healthy gulp, and the three of them sat on the street curb. Seventeen, he thought, that means something. It means I'm no kid anymore.

Billy Ray glanced over his shoulder at the mini-bus and noticed clouds of marijuana smoke drifting from a window.

"Do you really think he'll show—Elvis?" Billy Ray said.

"Why not?" Wino said. "He has to come home some time."

"Yeah, but you don't even know if he's in town. Maybe he's off doing a concert."

"Life's a crapshoot, Billy Ray." Wino chugged beer and kept an eye on Graceland.

"But if he shows, we'll be here."

"For how long? What about your drummer?"

"Until we decide we're pissing in the wind, Bobby Joe can wait. He'd understand what we're doing here."

"What are we doing here? You didn't come all the way from California just to see Elvis, did you?" He chugged more Dixie and had a decent buzz.

"We're sort of on a mission, Billy Ray," Wino said. "See Graceland, get inspired, pick up Bobby Joe, and become a band."

"And then hit New Orleans," Chess said. He raised his can of Dixie in salute. "The Big Easy."

Billy Ray grinned, touched his can to Chess's. "Are there gigs in New Orleans?"

He was nicely buzzed and accepted another Dixie from Chess.

"Bobby Joe's uncle owns a bar down there in the French Quarter," Chess said. "We can play for tips and bunk upstairs. It's doable."

"Groovy," Billy Ray said. He raised his can again. "To Gravy is Groovy."

"And uncles with bars," Wino said.

"To uncles," Billy Ray said, and his voice cracked just a little. Milt's face materialized then dissolved as quickly.

A car slowed down in front of Graceland and the three of them looked closely, but it was just a tourist slowing down for a gawk.

"Why New Orleans?" Billy Ray said after a while. "Why not Memphis? Or California?"

"Too crowded in California," Wino said. "Too many bands competing for the spotlight. Memphis is blues and country. So is New Orleans, except it's wide open down there. We don't want to become just another California band, Billy Ray. Sometimes you have to look beyond the horizon."

"I know exactly what you mean," Billy Ray said, realizing it was true, and that he was right to leave Argus. He just wasn't sure why it was necessary to worship at the Elvis Shrine. Helena, he knew from his map back home, was tantalizingly close. Less than a hundred miles, he figured.

"Is that why you're going to Helena, Billy Ray?" Wino said. "To look beyond the horizon? What about this uncle of yours?"

"Milt."

"Yeah, Milt. You say he died in Vietnam? Man, that's a shame. I'm sorry, Billy Ray."

"Thanks." Billy Ray drained his third Dixie and belched. "I didn't get to say goodbye to him, so I'm headed down to do that."

"What else?" Wino said.

"Well, I've got some family in Helena. My dad's from there. So was Milt. There's a bunch of cousins."

"Family's great, Billy Ray. So is saying goodbye. But let me put it this way—what do you want out of it?"

Billy Ray tossed his empty Dixie can in the cooler. What did he want?

Before Billy Ray could answer, squealing tires announced a pink Jeep. It lurched to a halt, and the driver examined Wino, Chess, and Billy Ray sitting on the curb.

"You boys lost?" Elvis Aaron Presley flashed his devastating grin. A shock of jet black hair danced on his forehead. He revved the Jeep's motor.

"Can you guys speak?" The King of Rock and Roll picked Billy Ray out of the thunderstruck trio. "How about you, son?"

Billy Ray got up slowly and stepped over to the Jeep. "I'm Billy Ray Fleener from Argus, Illinois."

"Are you now? Glad to meet you Billy Ray Fleener from Argus, Illinois." Elvis offered a hand and they shook.

"What are you boys up to?"

"We're a band," Wino said, his ability to speak restored. He and Chess crowded around the Jeep with Billy Ray.

It's really Elvis, Billy Ray thought, more impressed than he expected. Suddenly Graceland seemed magnificent to him.

"What's your band called?" Elvis said.

"We're called Gravy is Groovy." Wino winced after he said it.

Elvis got the sheepish look he often got in his movies when a girl initially rebuffed his advances. "That's what you call yourselves? Gravy is Groovy?"

"Well, yeah," Wino said. "What do you think?"

"Do you like it?" Elvis said. "Does it feel right, man?"

"I guess it does," Wino said, and Chess nodded agreement. The nearly-twins, who had appeared behind Billy Ray as silently as vampires, also nodded.

"Then, there you go," Elvis said, winking at the nearly-twins. "I gotta run, boys and girls." He revved the Jeep motor again.

"Do you have any advice for us?" Billy Ray said.

"Just be yourself, Billy Ray." Elvis flashed the grin again. "And take chances, man. Go to the edge and figure out what you want when you get there."

Elvis threw the Jeep in gear and gunned it through the opening gates and up the rise to his sanctuary.

Billy Ray decided he was ready for the edge, whatever that was.

# Three Confederate Generals

Billy Ray called his cousins from a gas station on the highway outside Helena. Then he said his goodbyes to Gravy is Groovy. He had a number for them in New Orleans, at the bar they'd be playing, and even the nearly twins urged Billy Ray to come to New Orleans for a visit.

"Don't settle for anything less than what you're looking for, Billy Ray," Wino said. He leaned out the window as they pulled away and flashed a peace sign. Billy Ray waved back and watched the mini-bus lumber down the highway south until it vanished. He felt sort of naked and vulnerable, but also pleased he had managed to get this far.

Soon a battered Ford pickup pulled into the station, and a boy about Billy Ray's age got out. He was a tad taller but thinner than Billy Ray and wore faded overhauls and a red baseball cap from his Little League days.

"You Billy Ray?"

"Yeah."

They shook hands awkwardly. Neither one quite knew what to say.

"Well, shit—hop in. I'm your cousin Taylor. Taylor Reeves."

Taylor gave Billy Ray the ten-cent tour.

"Over there's where they fought the Battle of Helena, Billy Ray." He pointed to hills anchoring the southern end of Crowley's Ridge. "Did you know about that?"

Billy Ray hadn't known, but nodded as if he did.

"Happened in eighteen something. I'm not real good at history. You know, the Civil War and all that."

"Right."

Taylor was just getting warmed up. "Here's another tidbit for you, man—there's three Confederate generals buried out in Maple Grove Cemetery."

"Really? Three? Amazing."

Billy Ray couldn't think of anyone at all from Argus who was famous or even noteworthy. "I had no idea Helena was so big in the war."

"You don't know the half of it," Taylor said, clearly pleased to impress his northern cousin. "Seven Confederate generals called Helena home. But just the three are planted out there."

"Groovy," Billy Ray said without thinking. Taylor shot him a funny glance, and they went along in silence for a while.

As they cruised into town Taylor fumbled with the radio.

"You want to hear King Biscuit?"

"What's King Biscuit?" Billy Ray said, vaguely thinking it must be some new band and wishing the name wasn't taken already because it sure beat Gravy is Groovy.

"King Biscuit is the blues station, Billy Ray. Been quite the deal since the 1930s or something. Maybe the 1940s. Helena's a blues town. Famous for it."

"Never heard of it."

"You got a lot coming to you, Billy Ray."

"I reckon I do." Billy Ray was tired of folks trying to teach him lessons. "So, do you work around here, Taylor?"

"The grain elevator. But I ain't no hayseed, if that's what you're thinking. Next year I'm going to Arkansas State up in Jonesboro to major in Ag."

"I wasn't thinking that at all, Taylor. We've got grain elevators in Argus, too."

"They say ours got burned down during the Civil War," Taylor said.

At the next stoplight Billy Ray reached over and turned the radio down.

"Look—maybe we could let the Civil War go. We don't have to fight it all over again—cuz."

Taylor threw the pickup in gear and gunned it down the street, but at the next light he turned to Billy Ray and grinned. "OK, cuz. Truce. I guess you've got a backbone in you after all."

"More than anybody knows. So, is there a good place to eat around here?"

"The VFW has good barbecue pork," Taylor said. "You want a beer?"

"Will they serve us there?"

"Shit, yeah. This ain't Illinois, Billy Ray. Folks are more relaxed down here. We go with the flow."

"Groovy," Billy Ray said, but this time Taylor didn't seem to mind.


A large and tattered Confederate battle flag hung on the wall behind the bar in the VFW. Other than that, Billy Ray noted that the Helena VFW was pretty much like the one back in Argus: a few pinball machines, walls dotted with pictures of men from various wars, and a sense of refuge from both the humidity and the outside world.

"Pretty hot down here," Billy Ray said. "More humid than back in Argus." He sipped the ice cold Dixie beer.

"Delta country, Billy Ray."

"And blues country." Billy Ray raised his can in salute. He didn't know shit about the blues, but figured it was good strategy with the locals and his cousins to be a fan, though he noticed the juke box was playing Patsy Cline.

"The blues," Taylor said, chugging his beer. "You know, Billy Ray, New Orleans isn't that far. This is the real south, cuz."

"I know it," Billy Ray said. "I came through Memphis."

Then Billy Ray told Taylor all about Gravy is Groovy and Elvis, and Taylor's eyes got big during the Elvis part.

"No shit? You met Elvis Fucking Presley? Hell, Billy Ray, I ain't never even been to Graceland. What did Elvis say?"

"Not much," Billy Ray said, enjoying leverage once again. "He said be yourself."

"Be yourself? That's all? You met Elvis and all he had to say was be yourself?"

Billy Ray sipped his Dixie slowly and drew the moment out for effect. He had Taylor on the edge of his bar stool.

"Let's see. Oh, yeah—he said go to the edge."

"Go to the edge?"

"That's right. Go to the edge and know what you want when you get there." Billy Ray patted Taylor on the shoulder for emphasis.

"The edge?" Taylor repeated as though repetition might reveal something. "Wow. That's deep alright."

"Simple elegance," Billy Ray countered. "Sometimes Milt said that about things."

With that opening, they finally confronted the subject both had avoided.

"Everybody down here was pretty broke up when Milt died," Taylor said. "I guess now we're all used to it. But nobody will forget him. Not ever."

"If he was here with us now," Billy Ray said, "he'd be the center of attention. People would buy him beers."

"Yes they would."

The sandwiches came, and they ate quietly for a while. Billy Ray thought it was the best barbecue he ever had. Even better than the Fourth of July pig roast in Argus.

"I was sick—tonsils," Billy Ray said suddenly after they ate. "That's why I didn't come down for the funeral."

"I heard. But now you're here to say goodbye, right"

"Yeah. At some point I knew I had to come."

"I can understand that," Taylor said. "Makes perfect sense to me."

Billy Ray told Taylor about his father, surfing, Beatle boots, and Moss.

"Your buddy Moss is in real trouble."

"I know it."

"Why do you suppose he done it?"

Billy Ray had finally worked that one out as far he could.

"He didn't mean to. Things just get to a point, and then there's no stopping them."

"That's God's own truth," Taylor said gravely. "Your pa sounds like he can be a beast sometimes. Do you think he'd ever hurt your ma?"

From someplace deep inside Billy Ray had become certain that wouldn't happen.

"He's a moralist. Well, that's what Milt called him once. Milt said moralists are all talk."

"I don't know anything about moralists, Billy Ray. Maybe he's just strict because he wants what's best for you."

"He has a funny way of showing it."

"I hear you," Taylor said. "Hey, I could get you on at the elevator if you want to stick around here."

"Really? Doing what?"

"Shoveling shit."

Billy Ray was tickled. "You're kidding, right?"

"I'm messing with you. That's what cousins are for, right?"

"I reckon," Billy Ray said. "Like when you gave me the treatment about the Civil War?"

"You're a Northerner, Billy Ray. We're family, so it's okay. But I just had to try you out—see if you had some balls."

"How'd I do?"

"You did okay, for a Yankee."

Billy Ray was pleased. He liked Taylor. With Moss in purgatory and no Get Out of Jail Free Card, Billy Ray was glad to have a friend.

"Milt said southerners are still fighting the Civil War. He said it was their peculiar burden."

Taylor nodded. "I reckon that's true enough, Billy Ray. But don't ask me to explain it. We lost and I guess it was hard to swallow. Even nowadays. Ain't we all fighting some war? You've got your Pa to deal with. Moss has his war, too."

"There was always something a little out of pocket with Moss,' Billy Ray said. "Now I see that."

"So, you want that job at the elevator? Mr. Turley is always hiring high school kids as he doesn't have to pay as much."

"I don't know. All I know right now is I have to go see Milt."

"Well, the offer's always good."

They ordered two more Dixies.

"Is it very far out to the cemetery?"

"Naw. Out by the river. They put Milt near those rebel generals. He's in good company, I suspect."

"Milt always liked other soldiers," Billy Ray said. "He liked hearing their stories."

"I'll take you out there when we're done."
The thought made Billy Ray suck in his breath.
"You've come a long way, Billy Ray."
"I reckon I have."

# 19

# Milt

Taylor waited in the truck.

Billy Ray found Milt's grave shaded by a tall poplar.

General Cleburne said, "Best view of the river."

General Hindman said, "No—better downstream."

General Tappan said, "Upstream. Better upstream."

General Hindman said, "General Cleburne is right."

General Tappan said, "You wouldn't know a good view."

General Cleburne said, "Still, the shade is good here."

General Tappan said, "Yes, we have good shade."

Milt said, "I'm dead, Billy Ray."

A breeze sprang up and ruffled the poplar's leaves. Tree limbs rubbed against each other and squeaked. The three Confederate generals had nothing more to say.

Billy Ray looked down at Milt's grave and remembered: the summer before Milt shipped out to Vietnam they drove to Chicago to see the Cubs. It was one of those cool Illinois summers that didn't drop in very often. But it was sunny and pleasant, and the drive north was a liberation from the confines of Argus and Fleener Hardware. Billy Ray was still but fifteen, and his lust for the peach fuzz on Margie Heinrich's tan thighs was only a future fantasy. It was the leg of the drive when they temporarily left the vast prairie stretching north of Bloomington for the rich, hilly Illinois River Valley that coated LaSalle and Ottawa and other river towns of tall church spires and sagging brown buildings squatting by the river.

"Are you scared, Milt?"

"Of what, Billy Ray?" Milt reached over and pinched Billy Ray's knee.

"Of Vietnam. Of dying."

Milt smiled, began to speak, but words didn't come out. He stared at the road a while. They had cleared the river valley, and it was flat prairie again. "We're trained not to fear."

Billy Ray pondered that. "Does it work?"

"Does what work?"

"Not being afraid."

"I hope so, Billy Ray." Then, more to himself than Billy Ray, "I hope so."

The Marines said Milt was killed in a river valley.

At the Cubs game Milt caught a foul ball that badly bruised his thumb. "See, Billy Ray? I'm wounded." Milt and Billy Ray laughed. The Cubs lost the game.

The Marines said Milt did not suffer.

On the drive back to Argus they saw several male pheasants malingering in a ditch by a corn field. Their bright colors were like the shiny medals on Milt's dress uniform. "It's a shame people shoot them," Milt said. "They're beautiful."

The Marines said Milt was a hero.

But Billy Ray knew different. Milt wasn't a hero. He wasn't a coward, either. He was a good man and a funny uncle, and Billy Ray had loved him as much as anyone, but he was no hero. He was just unlucky. He was honorable and honest and compassionate and liked a good squirt of bourbon, but he was unlucky. He understood a lot about people and places, and now Billy Ray knew with pride that Milt had passed some of that wisdom along to him; but Milt's wisdom was not enough to save him. He stepped in the wrong place in the wrong country at the wrong time and fate blew him a million miles in the air and reassembled him minus quite a few pieces near the muddy bank of a brown river.

The Marines were liars.

Billy Ray realized that Milt suffered. Even if he died quickly, he suffered. No one knew—or would say—how long he lived after he was blown up.

The Marines insisted he was a hero.

Another story: Billy Ray watched Milt pitch horseshoes one night at the VFW. Milt was quite good at it and could throw a ringer pretty often. The night air was cool, and it was a full moon. The VFW had turned on the lights out back, and the place seemed as bright as daylight. Many men of all ages were smoking cigars and reliving various wars and guzzling Stag and Falstaff beer. Milt won again, and he and Billy Ray adjourned to a picnic table. Billy Ray drank a Mountain Dew ,and Milt tossed back a shot of Very Old Barton, a hard to find bourbon from Kentucky, he claimed. One of the men, a veteran of Korea, had provided the bourbon.

"Where you're headed is a different kind of war, Milt," the Korea veteran said. "Nothing like what I saw in Korea."

"More like the Pacific in World War Two," Milt said.

The Korea veteran frowned. "Sure, it's a jungle war. But it's different than the Pacific, my friend."

"What do you mean?" Milt accepted another shot of Very Old Barton.

The Korea veteran shrugged his shoulders. "This one ain't a popular war. The enemy is always mingling with the civilian population. He might sell you a souvenir by day and shoot at you by night."

After the Korea veteran shuffled off with friends, Billy Ray asked whether Vietnam was worth the trouble.

"Not my job to decide that, Billy Ray."

"Milt?"

"Yeah, Billy Ray?

"Promise you'll be careful. Promise you'll be okay."

Milt looked a way for a moment. "I promise, Billy Ray. Don't you worry. Everything will be just fine."

Milt had promised. But Billy Ray knew that sometimes promises weren't possible to keep.

Something else controlled that.

The Marines said Milt followed procedures correctly. A hero, who didn't suffer.

The Marines were fools.

Billy Ray knew it was just bad luck. A crudely-designed mine manufactured in Hanoi had found its way to a river valley ,and the bottom of Milt's boot and erupted. The same power that steered the three Confederate generals to their graves under a shady poplar had delivered Milt into their company.

"Thanks for everything, Milt," Billy Ray said to the granite headstone. "I finally got here. I met my cousin Taylor—he's over by the truck. He's a good guy, even if he is kind of a hick. You were right—they're still fighting the Civil War down here. But it's okay. I get a kick out of hearing about it."

After a minute, he said, "Milt, I'm seventeen. I could join the Marines. But don't worry, I won't do that."

Billy Ray sat cross-legged in the grass. He wished he had brought some flowers. He would try and remember to do that the next time. In a letter from Vietnam, Milt had described beautiful flowers. Billy Ray scooted closer to the headstone.

"You know, I thought I'd know exactly what to say when I got here. But I don't. I guess there's really nothing to say except you meant so much to me, and I'm sorry about what happened to you in the A-Shau Valley."

Billy Ray had never quite been able to picture Moss shooting his father, but now he could vividly picture Milt dying, and it took him to a sad place very deep inside where his heart felt like it was in a tightening vise. Just as quickly it was released, and the image of Milt suffering slowly evaporated. Billy Ray experienced a flash of pain more searing than any serious cut or gash. It tumbled throughout his body like a bullet and then vanished.

Billy Ray had passed through a barrier he sensed he didn't have to try and understand. He looked over at the truck, at Taylor, who leaned against the cab and stared down at his tennis shoes.

"Thanks for everything, Milt. I love you, and I'll never forget you."

Billy Ray stood up. It was time to go. Milt was dead, and that was that. He had good men around him. He had company. Billy Ray understood it now, accepted it. Time to go.

Billy Ray shivered. Then calm filled him. He felt as light as a pheasant feather.

# 20

# The King Biscuit Flour Hour

In the fall, Billy Ray enrolled at Helena High School for his senior year and learned he had enough credits from Illinois and extra ones from the work/study program to graduate early and before Christmas. He had sprouted more than an inch, to six feet when wearing shoes, and his hair was over his collar. The Reeves family was an accommodating bunch happy to have him, they explained, because he reminded them of a younger version of Milt.

After school, Billy Ray worked a few nights at the grain elevator with Taylor—shoveling grain, which was not much different than shoveling shit, he noted. The work hardened his muscles.

Even Taylor was impressed. Mrs. Fleener took the train down for a visit that went pretty well, although she scarcely recognized him at first. She accepted his decision to stay in Helena and respected it, but seized the opportunity to promote several medical schools in the region. Mr. Fleener couldn't make the trip because he'd had what was at first thought to be a heart attack, but was instead just anxiety. His doctor advised rest and a hobby. Billy Ray figured his dad had finally been worn down some by all the vinegar in his veins.

For extra money, Billy Ray angled for a weekend job with The King Biscuit Flour Hour. The hour was indeed as famous as Taylor had claimed, and Billy Ray discovered an affinity for the blues. He figured he'd lived some of those blues already. So, Taylor introduced him one day down at the VFW to Tyler Jones, a King Biscuit producer, and when Tyler heard that Billy Ray claimed to know Elvis Presley, he gave him five minutes to sell himself for a job.

"Well, I did meet Elvis. That's true."

"Where? Where did you meet Elvis?"

"At Graceland. In Memphis."

Tyler grimaced slightly. "I know where Graceland is, son. I've met Elvis, too. What were the circumstances?"

"Circumstances?"

"How did you meet Elvis?"

"Oh. We were sitting outside Graceland, and he drove up in a pink Jeep and stopped to talk to us. We—"

"We?"

"Me and Gravy is Groovy. You see—"

"Gravy is Groovy? What's that?"

"They're a band. They play down in New Orleans."

"I see. What sort of band are they?

"Rock, and some blues, I think."

"Really? You do realize that here at King Biscuit we're always on the lookout for new blues talent. Is Gravy is Groovy any good? Have you heard them play, Billy Ray?"

Billy Ray chewed on that for an agonizingly long moment as he felt the heat of Tyler's stare. "They have a good guitar player. I heard him play."

"Some blues, Billy Ray? Did he play the blues?"

Billy Ray hesitated. "It was something by the Rolling Stones. From their latest album."

"The Rolling Stones? That's very good. And now this band of yours, they're playing in New Orleans?"

"But they're from California. Except the drummer—he's from Memphis."

"Really? A California band featuring a Memphis drummer, but performing in New Orleans. Intriguing."

"Wino said California was too crowded. He said the band needed to develop its own sound."

"Who is Wino?"

"Their guitar player. He's from San Francisco, I think."

"Ah, The Bay Area Sound." Tyler clasped his hands as though about to pray. He sank back in his chair and appeared lost in thought. When he came back to the world he said, "What you describe is all so very unique—a mixture of northern California, Memphis, and New Orleans. I'm not sure anyone has tried to blend those elements, those backgrounds. If they can play the blues, it might prove to be a new branch on the tree, if you will."

"A new branch?"

"A different direction for the blues."

"Groovy," Billy Ray said. "They also have two Cher look-alikes as their singers."

Tyler appeared flummoxed. "Good Lord and General Jackson," he said. "Twin female singers? And they look like Cher?"

Billy Ray shifted uneasily in his chair. "Not exactly like Cher. They remind you of Cher, though."

"Can they sing, my boy? Can they carry a tune? My goodness, throw in two women who can sing the blues with all that other stuff, and you have quite the exotic soup."

Billy Ray decided to roll the dice, "I'm their manager." It sounded strange to hear and surprised Billy Ray as much as

Tyler when it came out. "Well, sort of. I invested some money in them. I guess you'd say I'm one of their backers." Billy Ray felt a little ashamed that he had put so much elastic in the truth. But it was too late to take it back.

"You're a producer, Billy Ray." Tyler seemed to look at him in a whole new way.

"What's a producer?"

"In Hollywood, no one knows. It's a mystery, but it pays awfully well. In the music business, however, it's someone who takes a band by the hand—backed by cold hard cash—and leads them to the promised land."

"And what's the promised land, Mr. Jones?"

"Please, call me Tyler. The promised land is concerts, a record deal. Fame and glory, Billy Ray. Fame and glory."

Billy Ray said he was up for some fame and glory as much as the next guy.

Tyler rubbed his palms together greedily. "Excellent, my boy. Now the first thing is to arrange to see this Gravy is Groovy. What do you think of their name, Billy Ray?"

Billy Ray was smiling foolishly inside, but sober as a judge on the outside: "Well, Tyler, you've got your Moby Grape, your Jefferson Airplane, and your Buffalo Springfield. Those names stand out. So does Gravy is Groovy."

Tyler nodded gravely, one producer to another. "Spoken like a true producer, my boy. Excellent. The King Biscuit Blues Festival is coming up in October. Do you suppose we can get Gravy is Groovy up here for a looksee?"

"I don't see why not," Billy Ray said, wondering whether he even still had the piece of paper with the phone number for the band in New Orleans. He worried that perhaps he'd dug a hole too deep to get out of. Milt used to say that the man who dug the hole was the one most qualified to fill it up. But Milt also said you had to spread a little fertilizer if you wanted a garden.

After Tyler left, an attractive woman—rather voluptuous, Billy Ray thought—came in and sat at the end of the bar and ordered a vodka gimlet. She smiled at Billy Ray and licked her lips. She looked to be about 40, he thought, and had peroxide blonde hair. She wasn't gorgeous, but was far from average. Billy Ray thought she vaguely reminded him of Kim Novak or even Jayne Mansfield.

"Who is that?" Billy Ray quietly asked the bartender.

"That's Mrs. Southall," he said. "She works for you buddy, Tyler."

Billy Ray nodded and looked again at Mrs. Southall. She sure did seem to lick her lips a lot, he noticed. She smiled at him again and lifted her glass in salute.

When he left he felt sure he could feel her eyes on his back.

# 21

# The Big Easy

Early the next Saturday morning, Billy Ray and Taylor set off for New Orleans in Taylor's pickup to find Gravy is Groovy.

"This is crazy," Taylor said. "And I don't take it as promising that they didn't return your calls."

"They're musicians."

"Can't musicians return phone calls?"

"Musicians are too busy composing music. That's why they need managers."

"Do they know you're their manager?"

Billy Ray grinned. "Right now all that matters is that Tyler Jones thinks I am."

"And that this peckerwood band of yours can carry a tune, right?"

"And that, too."

Taylor tuned in King Biscuit on the radio, and the blues enveloped them.

"That's Robert Johnson," Billy Ray said. "I think." He was learning the blues thanks to Tyler Jones, who had said there was a difference between what the Rolling Stones played and what Robert Johnson played, but it was connected.

North of Lake Pontchartrain, they stopped at Luther Wilson's BBQ Shack and ate alligator sandwiches. Most of the patrons were negroes, but they paid little attention to Billy Ray and Taylor. Even Luther himself, tall and very black, came out from the kitchen wearing a sauce stained apron and took their orders.

"Tastes like chicken," Billy Ray said. "It's good, but what's the fuss about eating alligator meat?"

"Cause you can't just get it anywhere, I suppose. You won't find it up in Argus, Billy Ray."

"Maybe there's a reason for that." Billy Ray looked around the room. He recognized the sound coming from the jukebox as Motown—Aretha Franklin. Some negro boys and girls at a table by the jukebox clapped their hands softly to the beat. The girls had red ribbons in their hair. Taylor noticed Billy Ray surveying the room.

"There many negroes back in Argus?" He said it very softly and leaned toward Billy Ray.

Billy Ray thought it over and munched his sandwich.

"I don't think there's any at all. Not that I know of. There wasn't any at my school. You have to go to Bloomington-Normal, or over to Champaign, to find them."

"Part of the woodwork down here." Taylor said.

"Everyone seems to get along here," Billy Ray said.

Taylor looked around quickly. "Here, sure. The barbecue unites us. But there's places around here we can't go. Same for them." He said it as though he were discussing grain prices.

"Is that true back in Helena, too?"

"Sure it is, Billy Ray. But the blues festival evens that out some, I reckon.

"Is there a n— town in Helena?"

Taylor looked up sharply, then quickly at the nearest table. He reached over and grabbed Billy Ray's elbow. "Don't use that word here, Billy Ray." Taylor looked around again, but no one was watching. He released his grip on Billy Ray's elbow slowly.

They didn't say anything for a couple minutes.

Quietly, Billy Ray finally said, "But there is such a thing, right?"

"Yes," Taylor said, not looking up from his plate. "But you don't use that word in public. Down at the VFW, it's different. But not here." Taylor looked away, then back with a frown. "Did you learn about stuff like that that down here, or bring it with you from Argus?"

"I heard it at the VFW, in Helena."

Taylor nodded. "That's where you'll hear it, alright."

"Milt said they were just like us, but different, Taylor. What do you suppose that means?"

"I don't know. Sometimes Milt was full of shit."

Billy Ray bristled. "Not about important things he wasn't."

Taylor saw the heat in Billy Ray's eyes. "You're right, Billy Ray. I do apologize."

"Accepted." Billy Ray finished his iced tea. "Milt told me they don't want to be called negroes anymore. Blacks. They want to be known as blacks. What do you think?"

Taylor looked around to make sure no one was listening. "I think people ought to be called what they want. Let's talk about something else, Billy Ray."

"Like what?"

"You ever been to a hootchy-koochy show?"

"They have one of those every year at the McLean County Fair," Billy Ray said. "They wouldn't let me and Moss in. Milt went all the time and let one of the girls wear his marine cap."

"Sounds like Milt. Well, New Orleans ain't McLean County, Billy Ray. They'll let just about anyone in who looks old enough."

"Do we look old enough?"

"Hell yes, we do."

They found the French Quarter and parked near the Hotel Monteleone. To Billy Ray the quarter was a melting plot of old and young, black and white, carefree hippies openly smoking pot and world-weary proprietors with fake smiles.

"We could get high just standing near all the hippies," Billy Ray said.

"That's a fact. You ever smoke pot, Billy Ray?"

"No. Have you?"

"Sure I have," Taylor said. "But we have to keep that between the two of us. Helena's a tightass Republican town."

"So's Argus. Look at those two guys over there. Smoking right out here in the open."

Billy Ray looked around for police, but didn't see any. He couldn't believe how open it was.

"Don't point for Christ's sake, Billy Ray. When we get back to Helena we'll have to fire up a doobie."

Billy Ray laughed out loud. Did everyone in the universe know what a doobie was before he did?

"In school they said marijuana will make you go insane."

"That's just FBI propaganda," Taylor said. "You don't believe that shit, do you."

Billy Ray hesitated. "I guess I don't. But teachers ain't supposed to lie to you."

"They lie all the damn time," Taylor said. "Dope's just like beer, only different. Do those two guys look insane?"

Billy Ray studied them. They seemed relaxed to the point of becoming liquid. "No, they look kind of happy."

"That's because they're stoned to the gills."

They drifted over to Royal Street and located the hootchy kootchy place, Taboo Inn.

A ham-faced man wearing a Hawaiian shirt was out front bellowing, "The quarter's prettiest girls, right here. Step inside for the time of your life."

Inside it was so dark that Billy Ray felt blind. For a moment he worried that he had inhaled marijuana smoke and blindness was a delayed effect. Then their eyes adjusted, and they found a table. Armed with a couple Dixie beers, they waited for the prettiest girls in the quarter.

What they got were the most bored-looking girls in the quarter.

"Could her tits droop any lower?" Taylor said as a blonde passed by.

Billy Ray, suddenly recalling his lust for Margie Heinrich, was far less critical. "They look pretty good to me."

"That's because you northern boys would screw a snake if someone held its mouth open."

They clanked beer cans in salute, spilling a good amount. Billy Ray had a brief, disturbing image of his penis in a snake's mouth. "Like you southern boys wouldn't fuck a snake if someone held its mouth open."

"Not a live one, dickhead."

One of the girls wiggled her butt in Billy Ray's face, but Billy Ray declined to purchase a lap dance. He still wasn't entirely clear on all the different ways a guy could get VD.

"I think my pants are on fire," he said.

"That's why they keep a fire extinguisher over there on the wall."

"You know," Billy Ray said, "it's amazing you boys lost the war, what with your great wit and all."

Taylor chuckled. "It's amazing you boys won it, what with screwing live snakes and such."

Taylor bought a lap dance from a brunette with very pink, erect nipples. "Who's the loser now?" he yelled.

After the brunette lurched off in search of new prey, Billy Ray was beside himself about her nipples.

"That's the air conditioning," Taylor said. "They keep it cranked to make their nipples hard."

"It's working."

When Billy Ray came back from the men's room, he noticed that the little stage in a corner of the cavernous bar had amplifiers and guitars on it. He was reminded of their mission to find the band and stopped Taylor from buying yet another lap dance. As they were leaving, a band took the stage.

It was Gravy is Groovy.

"Holy shit, Taylor, that's them."

"That's Gravy is Groovy? Man, you didn't say it was a titty bar they played in. What a sweet deal."

Wino, Chess, the nearly-twins, and the black drummer, Bobby Joe were on stage sipping beers, laughing, checking equipment.

Then they launched into "Midnight Hour," a song Billy Ray had recently added to his growing list of cool songs. Billy Ray was pleasantly surprised. Gravy is Groovy was good. Even the nearly-twins were decent singers, and Wino added a gravelly but appealing voice Billy Ray thought was a little like CCR's John Fogarty— another recent acquisition. Bobby Joe's hands were a blur with the drumsticks, and Chess picked nimbly at a Hofner violin bass. Billy Ray knew the Hofner was what Paul McCartney played.

Gravy is Groovy was a real band, playing real music. They even did "Get Off My Cloud."

After the set, Billy Ray tipped a dancer to take him backstage.

"Jesus H. Christ," Wino said. "It's Billy Ray Damn Fleener."

The nearly-twins gave Billy Ray a group hug. He slapped palms with Chess and Bobby Joe.

Billy Ray didn't know what to say, so he blurted out, "You were great."

"Did you doubt us?" Wino said. "Man, how'd you like our version of Get Off Of My Cloud?"

"It was slower than the Stones, but good."

"Yeah, well, it wouldn't hurt to have Mick Jagger when we do that one, but we're learning. How in the world did you find us? We never heard from you, Billy Ray."

"I called. I left messages."

"No one gives messages around here. This joint is pretty much up for grabs."

"This is the first place we tried," Billy Ray said. "My cousin Taylor knew it. He's outside."

"It must be fate or karma or something," Wino said. "Look, about your fifty dollars—we didn't forget that. It's just money is kind of slow down here. We can give you half of it now."

"That's not why I'm here, Wino. I've got a proposition for you. Does that sound familiar?"

"Jesus, man—that's what I said to you in that funky diner in Saint Louie. What sort of proposition?"

"Back in Helena. I'm working with the King Biscuit radio station."

"King Biscuit?" Bobby Joe said. "You work with those guys? Man, I grew up on King Biscuit."

"Yeah, I've heard of King Biscuit," Wino said. "Can you get us a gig with them? Can we record something that they'll play?"

"That's what I'm trying to tell you. I told one of the producers about you, and they want to hear you play."

"No fucking shit?"

"No shit. I told them I was your manager."

Wino thought about it a moment. "Well, we better have a vote on that. This band is democratic. Everybody who wants Billy Ray as our manager, raise your hand."

They all raised their hands. The nearly-twins raised both their hands.

"Then you're our manager, Billy Ray. Of course, we get to keep the fifty."

"Of course."

Wino offered his hand and noted Billy Ray was different—taller, perhaps. "You've come a long way, Billy Ray."

"I know it."

# 22

# Rolling a Doobie

They hiked up one of the smaller hills of Crowley's Ridge. Billy Ray and Taylor could see the river and the far shore of Mississippi. The Battle of Helena had been fought all around them, and Billy Ray was trying to imagine it while also learning to roll his first marijuana cigarette.

"Like this," Taylor said. He sprinkled some pot into the paper and rolled it expertly between his index fingers and thumbs into a joint. "I learned watching my dad roll real cigarettes."

"Why do they call them doobies?" Billy Ray examined the finished product.

"Damned if I know, Billy Ray. They just do. They call them by lots of names."

Billy Ray looked off into the distance, where the Confederate line had been.

"That's what I'm discovering about life, Taylor. Things exist sort of like they're electrical outlets. No one quite knows how they got there, but they plug into them all the same."

Taylor lit the joint, inhaled slowly and held it for five seconds. He expelled a gray cloud and then passed the joint to Billy Ray.

"Damn, Billy Ray, you ain't supposed to make those deep as shit comments until after you're stoned."

Billy Ray inhaled, but coughed immediately. He did it over and had more success. Taylor handed him a Dixie from the cooler. Billy Ray took a gulp. He tried the joint again and managed it, holding the smoke in and then expelling fairly smoothly.

"How long does it take?" he said.

Taylor accepted the joint. "It's different for everyone. But not long, I reckon."

They passed the joint until it was nearly gone.

"They call this tiny part a roach, Billy Ray."

More education, Billy Ray noted. "What do we do with that? Just toss it?"

"Nope. We fire it up and snort it." Taylor pulled out his Swiss army knife and placed the roach in the teeth of the knife's folding scissors.

"I had no idea how handy this knife would be when I got it for my birthday."

He put it under Billy Ray's nose, and Billy Ray snorted like a pig.

After a while, Billy Ray could see the Confederate line advancing, battle flags flapping.

"I can see the Confederate flag—right over there."

Taylor snickered. "Yup—you're stoned."

"Really? Do I look stoned?"

"Yes, you do."

"I guess, I am. I feel funny, but good. It's pretty different."

"Mellow," Taylor said. "And you haven't gone insane yet, like your teachers predicted."

"There's still time."

They both laughed.

Later Billy Ray thought about Moss, gone off to prison. He tried not to think of Milt, but it was hard.

"What do you think about the war, Taylor?"

Taylor got them two more ice cold Dixies.

"The war's over. You guys won and get to screw live snakes. To the victors go the spoils and all that"

Billy Ray laughed until he drooled. "Sorry, man." He dabbed his chin with the bottom of his t-shirt.

"Not that war, dickhead. The other one—Vietnam. When we turn eighteen, they can draft us, right?"

Taylor was amused. "Not until we graduate high school. By then you'll be a big time music producer, and I'll be your assistant. They won't draft big shots like us."

"Sure they will," Billy Ray said. "Aren't you worried?"

"Nope. I've been accepted up at ASU. Student deferment."

"But if they did, would you go? I hear some guys run off to Canada."

"I don't think I could do that," Taylor said after a while. "I wouldn't be able to come back to Helena if I did."

Billy Ray watched a barge crawling along the river, headed south for New Orleans.

Gravy is Groovy would be arriving in a few days from New Orleans. He had a fleeting thought of the band arriving on a barge while playing. Pretty good promotion, he thought.

Maybe a photo in the Helena Gazette.

"Earth to Billy Ray." Taylor was giggling. "Man, you spaced there for a while. Where'd you go, man?"

Billy Ray felt a little pot paranoia creep over him for the first time. "Nowhere special. I was just thinking." He struggled to re-connect to their conversation. Everything had slowed down. "Oh, yeah. Like I was saying—would it be wrong to go to Canada?"

Taylor watched the barge, too. "I don't know, man. It's a choice. I'll tell you what I remember from history class: in the Civil War, you could pay someone to take your place. Except for the most part, only rich dudes could come up with the money."

"Figures. Milt didn't have that option."

"Milt was a marine, Billy Ray. Nobody twists your arm to join them Marines. He knew what he was doing. Like I said, it was a choice."

Billy Ray shook his head. "That's just it. I don't think he did. I don't think he really knew what it was all about. Milt bought in to the uniform and the image of marines. John Wayne and all that macho shit. We weren't even in the war when he joined up. He didn't mean to go to a war. He didn't mean to get killed."

Taylor frowned. "So why'd he join, smart guy?"

Billy Ray frowned, too. "To get out of town, man. Just to get out of town."

Taylor chugged his can of Dixie.

"He sure got out of town, Billy Ray. He got himself way out of damn town."

"Yeah, he did." Billy Ray stood up, though it took some effort.

"And I won't make the same mistake. C'mon, Taylor—let's go the VFW. I'm so hungry I could eat a horse."

"Yup—you're stoned alright."

# 23

# Working with Mrs. Southall

Gravy is Groovy left a phone message with Mrs. Southall, who had coordinated the Helena Blues Festival for ten years.

"Someone named Wino," She said to Billy Ray. "They'll be here tomorrow."

"Outstanding," Billy Ray said, relieved to know Wino could be reliable. He noticed that Mrs. Southall had a small mole in the crevice where her cleavage began. She handed him a stack of posters.

"These need to go up anywhere you can put them, Billy Ray, but make sure there's plenty of them where people congregate—bars, restaurants. When you run out, come back, and I'll find some more for you."

She licked her lips.

Billy Ray had never seen lipstick quite so red—cherry red, though cherry wasn't a word to associate with Mrs. Southall. She cocked her head as though expecting him to say something, but he just smiled and grabbed the posters. He looked over his shoulder going out the door, and she was still watching him.

He went to the Piggly Wiggly grocery store first because it was right across the street. Billy Ray wasn't convinced that putting up posters was what producers really did, but he was getting paid and seeing the town. There was a cute blonde cashier at Piggly Wiggly named Lucy, who was in his English class. She reminded him a little of Margie Heinrich, but now he couldn't decide if that was good or bad. She wasn't working, so Billy Ray bought an RC Cola and sat outside.

It got cloudy, but Billy Ray managed to distribute posters at Rexall's and the Woolworth store before the rain fell. He holed up under an awning at the John Deere dealer. The rain smelled fresh and clean. When it slowed to drizzle he worked his way down to the docks and put up more posters. He could see rain falling in sheets on the Mississippi. Thunderclaps drummed off in the distance. He could barely make out a tug maneuvering a barge along the far side of the river.

Billy Ray felt injected with something pretty elemental—raw energy, perhaps. He felt cleansed and alive and without worry as he allowed the drizzle to soak his t-shirt and run down his face. In the men's room at the diner on the docks, he dried his hair and face with paper towels and stayed to eat some french fries. He was at the confluence of an awful lot of things: Gravy is Groovy, high school graduation—he'd discovered he had enough credits to finish in December—and his eighteenth birthday, just a week away.

He ran out of posters and headed back downtown. The rain had left pools in the street gutters. Billy Ray took off his shoes and socks and rolled up his jeans for the walk back. The water was cool and refreshing. Five blocks later he put his shoes and socks back on so he could cut through Ike's Tavern, which had a back door to the alley behind the King Biscuit station.

Ike's was nearly empty except for a pair of gritty tug pilots drinking shots of Wild Turkey at the bar. That was probably their tug he saw tied to the docks. Ike, a generous contributor to the blues festival, nodded at him while wiping beer glasses.

There were a couple greaser types—high school dropouts still sporting pompadours and long sideburns—shooting pool. The juke box played something Billy Ray recognized as Merle Haggard, but he didn't know the title. He wasn't much for Merle Haggard. Sitting at the end of the bar Mrs. Southall nursed a vodka gimlet.

Billy Ray considered a hasty retreat back through the front, but Mrs. Southall had clearly seen him. She waved him over and patted the bar stool next to her.

"Done already? My, you're a fast worker, Billy Ray. What's yours? Ike, bring this hard working boy something to drink."

Billy Ray ordered a Dr. Pepper thinking it was best to keep beer drinking and his professional life separate. Mrs. Southall ordered a second gimlet and excused herself to visit the ladies room. Ike glanced over at Billy Ray a couple times and made him feel uncomfortable. He was thankful when the tug pilots ordered another round, and Ike was busy again.

Mrs. Southall came back chipper and refreshed and sipped her gimlet. Billy Ray couldn't be sure, but he thought there was one more button undone on her blouse. She had sprayed on more perfume. He noticed that as soon as she sat back down. It vaguely reminded him of his mother's perfume, which was sort of creepy in an equally vague way. But Mrs. Southall didn't look like his mother. Mrs. Southall had curves the tight dress accentuated. She had breasts that got noticed. She made sure of that.

"I'll go get some more posters, Mrs. Southall," he said. "It stopped raining."

"Call me Ruth, Billy Ray. Will you do that for me?"

Billy Ray nodded. "I guess so. Ruth."

"Mercy, we've worked together all these months, and it's always Mrs. Southall this and Mrs. Southall that, Billy Ray.

It's enough to make a southern lady feel like she's become a grandmother."

Billy Ray wasn't sure what to say to that so he sipped the Dr. Pepper and nodded every now and then. He didn't think any man who saw her cleavage thought much about grandmothers. He was pretty sure she had unbuttoned another button of her blouse, and he was getting a pretty good view of the fleshy tops of Mrs. Southall's titties. He imagined her giving a lap dance at the Taboo Inn and shaking those titties in his face. Thinking of them as titties instead of breasts made him excited. He felt the old sex salami shift a little in his underpants.

"Don't fret about those posters, honey. The rain's going to pick up again, anyway. It usually does. You can start where you left off in the morning, before your band gets here."

"I reckon so, Ruth." If she minded him looking her titties over she gave no hint of it.

She cocked her head like she generally did and regarded him a moment. "What kind of name is Gravy is Groovy? I swear to the heavens I never heard such a thing."

"It's just what they came up with to stand out."

"Can they play, Billy Ray? Tyler Jones don't like to be disappointed. It's a feather in your cap if they can play." She got herself another gimlet. "You sure you don't want a beer or something, honey? You do drink beer don't you?"

"Sometimes. But I'm working." Working at not falling into her cleavage, he thought.

"You're off the clock now, Billy Ray. Have a beer. Ike, bring this young man a beer. I'm calling you a young man because you are. I hear tell your eighteenth birthday is coming up."

He waved the beer off, and Ike nodded. Mrs. Southall was at the point of not really noticing.

"I remember when I turned eighteen," she said. "I went off to a dance school in Biloxi. That's where I met Mr. Southall. He played piano in a band there."

No one that Billy Ray talked to seemed to know what happened to Mr. Southall and Mrs. Southall didn't volunteer to enlighten him. She drank another gimlet. "I was quite the dancer, I'll have you know." She fished in her purse and found some change. "Here. Go play G5."

He discovered that G5 was "I Can't Stop Loving You" by Ray Charles.

Mrs. Southall ambushed him at the juke box. She slipped her arms around him from behind. "Dance with me, Billy Ray."

Billy Ray only knew a two-step he learned in dance class in school. Mrs. Southall pressed her titties into him, and the sex salami started having evil thoughts. A couple girls back in Argus had choked his chicken for him, but he had yet to perform under the main tent. And this wasn't the time or place. Ike was eyeing him closely behind the bar. Mrs. Southall had ground her pelvis into Billy Ray's crotch, and Ike wasn't too sure about it all. This was the middle of the day and not a crowded dance floor on a Saturday night.

Bill Ray took the hint and steered Mrs. Southall back to finish her gimlet.

When she fumbled for her car keys and declared she didn't really think she should drive and would Billy Ray help out a gal, he knew he was finally going to get where he had wanted to go ever since Margie Heinrich's peach fuzz thighs had appeared before him.

For Ike's consumption, he made a point of saying he'd help Mrs. Southall get back to the office, but Ike wasn't buying it, and his look said so. Billy Ray figured his sex life would become an item in Helena. But what's a guy to do? It's a choice and Billy Ray had made it. A guy had to do what a guy had to do. Billy Ray simply couldn't turn eighteen and still be a virgin. And Mrs. Southall was happy to help him out.

He had to practically pour Mrs. Southall out of her car when they reached her house.

But she perked up when they got there and even made them vodka gimlets. He liked them well enough. She even surprised him by playing some Beatles before slipping on Frank Sinatra to dance to. Dancing was a very loose way of regarding it. He had the boner of his life trying to burst his zipper, and Mrs. Southall was more than happy to two-step and show good dexterity at the same time by slipping off her dress and releasing his feverish salami to roam at will.

On the couch in her living room she straddled him, and the penetration made him actually gasp. He had no idea what he had been missing. It was like thrusting into something wet and velvet and appreciative and warm and and and and quickly he couldn't even think of it in terms of words, and he just met her grinding hips with his own thrusts and lost his sense of time and place. There was nothing but where his penis was and what his penis was doing.

He came too quickly, of course, and it was a dike breaking under a hurricane, but she reassured him everything would be just fine.

"That's just the first inning, honey. Rome wasn't built in a day."

In her bedroom, she brought him back to life, and the game went into extra innings.

Later, while Mrs. Southall primped in the bathroom, Billy Ray asked himself how in the world Margie Heinrich could have done it any better.

# 24

# Everything on the Line

Being a band manager, Billy Ray discovered, meant mostly calming the nerves of the band as it waited for it's most important gig. It was the second day of the festival, and Gravy is Groovy was slotted to perform last. He employed one of his newest skills and expertly rolled a doobie for the band to circulate.

"Thanks, man." Wino passed the joint around. The band was quiet. Everyone had their own routine for the wait: Chess tuned and re-tuned his bass, Bobby Joe twirled a drumstick absently, The nearly-twins combed each other's hair, Wino chewed on his guitar pick.

Billy Ray basked in the glow of porking Mrs. Southall. He'd gotten his ashes hauled good and properly. Mrs. Southall even made him breakfast the next morning—waffles, bacon and eggs, juice and coffee. For good measure, they went another nine innings.

He declined the joint. His high was pretty natural at the moment. Pot was fine, but he didn't think he was destined to become a pot head. And a clear head was best for this day.

"You'll all do fine," he told the band. "You sounded great in New Orleans."

A little tune-up was all they needed. Some cheerleading to get them motivated.

Wino grimaced. "This ain't a titty bar, Billy Ray. That's a real audience out there, and they know their music."

Well, maybe there was more to being a manager than Billy Ray figured. He also didn't appreciate the rebuke, mild as it was. What would Milt call it? Insubordination? But anger wasn't called for. Finesse was. Billy Ray figured he'd picked up finesse along with all his other lessons.

He decided to quell the dissent before the troops became unmanageable.

"All the better, Wino. Did you drive all the way from California to fail?"

"No, but—"

"No damn butts, man." Billy Ray wouldn't give an inch. "Time to suck it up and show what you have."

"Easy for you to say."

No more, Billy Ray decided. The buck stops here. "In case you didn't notice, mister lead guitar player, I'm on stage here, too. I got Tyler Jones to give you a tryout. My reputation's on the line, too."

Billy Ray was amused. Did he even have a reputation to be put on a line? By God, maybe he did.

The band digested it. No one said anything for a minute. Then Bobby Joe abruptly stood up. "The man's right, Wino. We wouldn't be here if it wasn't for Billy Ray."

"This is what we worked so hard for," Chess said. "It's our shot, man."

Wino's grimace slowly turned into a grin. He'd bought it. Billy Ray really was their manager. At least for this day. And he liked being called a man. Confidence surged through Billy Ray. And maybe a little anger, too. After all the trouble he'd gone to, he decided he wasn't about to let the band go to pieces. Billy Ray had been looking for a cause, something to sink his teeth into. Something that said Billy Ray Fleener left his mark here. This was as good as any, he figured. He knew that he wasn't a music producer. Fifty dollars in gas money didn't bestow that. But he sensed he could be one if that's what he decided. He was no longer afraid to try.

"I'm not a musician," Billy Ray said. He had their attention. "But I know what sounds good. I can tell the difference between shit and talent. I heard talent that day in New Orleans. Gravy is Groovy belongs here, on this stage. Now go out there when it's your damn turn and be Gravy is Groovy."

Tyler Jones beckoned Billy Ray to sit with him in the stands. Gravy is Groovy was up next. There had been some early morning showers, but now the sun was brilliant. Billy Ray took that as a good sign. He looked around. The stands were pretty full. It was a noisy crowd, fortified with beer and barbecue. They had heard good music from the first and would demand no less from the last.

"Is this band of yours ready, Billy Ray? Will we be getting their A game today?"

Tyler Jones was known to be a shrewd judge of talent. But a difficult man to please. He could make a band, and Billy Ray supposed, could break one, too. Fame and glory, the man had said. Fame and glory.

"They'ready." Billy Ray sipped Dixie beer from a cup.

"Playing your cards close to the vest?" Tyler Jones said.

Shifting responsibility, perhaps, was what Billy Ray figured he was doing. Everybody did it to a degree. "It's out of my hands, TJ. I had a little chat with them, and now it's up to them to be who they are."

"Spoken like a true producer, Billy Ray. Isn't that what Elvis advised—be yourself?"

Producer. Billy Ray chewed on that. "That's what the man said. That's what I told them backstage. But you can't put a backbone in a man, TJ. He has to do that for himself."

Tyler Jones raised his eyebrows. "How old are you again, Billy Ray?"

"Eighteen in a couple days."

"He's eighteen going on thirty-five," said Taylor, who plopped down next to Billy Ray.

"Sorry I'm late—there was an extra truck to load at the elevator."

"You're just in time," Billy Ray said. "There they are."

Gravy is Groovy popped out from backstage, stared stonily for a moment at the crowd, and then took possession of the stage. Clearly they wanted it. Bobby Joe twirled both drumsticks and grinned from ear to ear. Chess jutted his jaw out as though daring the crowd not to notice him. The nearly-twins were like two swaying palm trees. Wino clutched his Les Paul like it was a machine gun.

Billy Ray had a good feeling.

"Too late to run," Taylor whispered.

"I ain't going anywhere. Just watch."

"Moment of truth, my boy," Tyler Jones said, but he, too, sensed the confidence and noticed the band's swagger. To him they looked like they wanted it pretty bad. They were a hungry band and it showed.

First up was "Midnight Hour" to get them warmed up. They mixed blues and rock because Gravy is Groovy wasn't fully the blues and not fully rock. The band hovered nicely and comfortably in the middle and borrowed from each end and somehow made it seem their own.

Their secret, Billy Ray concluded, was in not straying too far from inspired competence and to rely on Wino's gravelly voice to be an interesting counterpoint to the more velvety voices of the nearly twins. Truth was, Wino could play lead. He wasn't Jimi Hendrix or Eric Clapton but he was fluid enough to lead the band. And he had paid attention to the blues axmen who paved the way. Chess was solid on bass, Bobby Joe had flair and was a great timekeeper on drums, and the nearly-twins were that visual treat Wino bragged about. Gravy is Groovy would never mangle a song by drifting too far away from the original version, and yet, they gave the impression of adding to every song some seasoning that was their own. Competence times substance and gimmick equals success, Wino had told Billy Ray.

The set was seamless. One song melted into the next. There was no drifting, no fumbling, and he crowd stayed with them. They were a hit and knew it. The crowd erupted when it was over.

Gravy is Groovy strutted the stage. They even did an encore by request.

"Thank-you," Wino said. "We're going to close with one for our manger, Billy Ray Fleener." Wino pranced to the front of the stage. "There he is—stand up, Billy Ray."

Billy Ray did stand up, and the crowd cheered lustily. He knew most of them were drunk, but still it was pretty cool.

Wino was back at his microphone: "The last time we did this one, Billy Ray said we were a little slow. He was right. But we've been practising since then."

And so Gravy is Groovy punctuated a great audition with a dead-on "Get Off My Cloud." Mick Jagger might have been proud.

Rain began falling lightly, but no one seemed to care.

All that was left for Billy Ray to do was take a bow himself later that night at Ike's.

The whole King Biscuit crowd was there except Mrs. Southall, who had a festival to close. Gravy is Groovy shot pool in the back room as a way to come back down to earth.

As always, Tyler Jones got to the point: "You delivered, Billy Ray."

"It was all them," he said, pointing to the pool tables. But he felt very connected to it. It was a good feeling.

"I know a small label that would likely be interested in them," Tyler said. "They can stand some polish here and there, but they have talent. You can't teach talent. You either have it or you don't."

"Thanks, TJ."

"It's not a huge label, mind you. But for Gravy is Groovy it's a nice vault up the food chain. Good job, Billy Ray. Come by the station tomorrow."

Billy Ray felt like he'd fallen into a barrel of tits and had come up sucking them all. Taylor reached over and patted Billy Ray on the shoulder.

"You did good, Cuz."

Billy Ray watched Gravy is Groovy shoot pool. Even the nearly-twins were into it.

The balls made loud smacks, and a few flew off the tables. Chess played air bass with his pool cue. Wino lined up a shot while Bobby Joe tried to distract him by twirling a drumstick.

"You better tell them about the record label, Billy Ray," Taylor said. "They sure earned it."

But Billy Ray knew there was no hurry. He understood what Milt might say about the band: like soldiers who performed well and survived a crucial test, they needed this time to revert back to innocence and cool off. Victory, especially a first victory, could be pretty damn hard to swallow. There was plenty of time to tell them what they already knew: they'd proven themselves under fire.

Billy Ray knew he had proven himself, too. To a degree, anyway. But still he was happy. Happy especially for Gravy is Groovy, which really did deserve the break. They had stepped up and earned it. And because of it, he was practically a Helena celebrity. But he also reminded himself that fate or karma or just plain old luck had played a big role and he said so.

Tyler Jones replied that luck and fate visited many people, but stayed to visit only with those who embraced it. He predicted Billy Ray could become the youngest music producer he'd ever heard of with a little more experience and some guidance. Taylor added that Billy Ray could be just about anything if he put his mind to it.

And yet strangely enough, Billy Ray's level of satisfaction was already eroding. Inevitably victory cooled and reality set in. He hadn't thought much about things beyond Gravy is Groovy, and now he did, and a truth finally descended on him like a blanket: Gravy is Groovy was moving up and would be in the hands of professionals. They didn't need him anymore. They didn't know it yet, but soon they would see it. There just wasn't much else Billy Ray could do for them except be a sort of cheerleader—or worse, a mascot. A lucky charm. The band would feel bad, of course, when they realized there would need to be a change, but in the end, Billy Ray believed, they would accept a change was necessary. The same strength that gave them the gumption to be a hit at the festival would fuel them to accept that Billy Ray had no role to play any more beyond friendship. Wino and the rest were good people and liked him, Billy Ray believed, but they were soldiers, too, ready to face the realities of their struggle.

So on a night with victory so fresh, one he undeniably had a hand in, Billy Ray demonstrated that he had learned one of the most powerful lessons of his young life. Knowing he wouldn't be moving on with the band, he chose to keep the epiphany to himself and not tarnish the night for Gravy is Groovy. He didn't even tell Taylor.

There was plenty of time left for good byes.

# 25

# Birthday

There was a cake.
And eighteen candles.
Punch and cookies and ice cream, too.
And the Reeves family crowded around him.
A card and a phone call from his mother.
Eighteen.
Billy Ray relished it.
Needed it.
It had taken a while to sink in.
Wow—eighteen!
He blew out the candles.
Made a wish.
Gravy is Groovy paid back the fifty dollars.
Taylor gave him a framed picture of Milt in dress blues.
And a case of Dixie beer.
Mrs. Southall jumped his bones one more time.
He was a man.
Youngest festival producer ever.
Lucy at Piggly Wiggly flirted with him
Tyler Jones offered him a full-time job when he graduated.

Everyone wanted to know what he wished for.
But Billy Ray kept that to himself.

# 26

# Ghost

A newly-minted high school graduate, Billy Ray did indeed feel different. Not older, but definitely a little wiser. Seasoned was the word, he decided. Weathered, too. He went out to Crowley's Ridge alone one last time and sat on a tree stump and looked out over the river. It was a cold winter for that part of the delta, and he could see his breath. Snow was coming. When Milt's image appeared, he tried to ignore it at first.

"You're not real," Billy Ray said.

"Real as real gets, Billy Ray."

"I'm not really seeing you."

"Seeing is a very fluid concept," Milt said. "Especially at my end."

"But you're not really there, Milt. Here, I mean."

"Then where am I, Billy Ray?"

"Heaven."

"Does that mean I can't be here, too?"

"How should I know," Billy Ray said. "I'm not the one who's dead. You can be here and heaven at the same time?"

"Heaven is everywhere, Billy Ray."

"Thanks a lot. That really helps me out."

"If it was easy, it wouldn't be a mystery."

"Are you really there, Milt?"

"I'm in your head, son. This is just how you choose to view me. It's all up to you, really."

"Are you here to haunt me?"

"There's really no such thing. That's a widespread misconception."

"But people see ghosts, right?"

"Do they?"

"You have to help me out here a little, Milt. This is new to me."

"Me, too, Billy Ray. I'm just getting the hang of it. I haven't been dead all that long."

"Don't they give you a training manual or something?"

"That would be helpful, alright. Like I said, I'm in your head. How I appear and where is up to you."

"So, I could put you anywhere, is that it?" Billy Ray said. "How about down by the river mooning grain barges?"

"Up to you, son. It would sure bring back memories, that's for sure."

"Milt, am I hallucinating?"

"Do you think you are, Billy Ray?"

"No, I don't think so. Maybe I'm daydreaming."

"Dreams are part of reality, Billy Ray."

"But you're in heaven, right, Milt?"

"Heaven's just a word."

"I thought you said heaven was everywhere?"

"It's both—it's everywhere and just a word."

Billy Ray stood up and walked a few yards. He turned back to Milt.

"You'll follow me?" Billy Ray said.

"I'll go wherever you want, son. Or not at all. I can disappear and come back later. Tomorrow. Next week. Next year. In fifty years. It's all up to you."

"Are we really having a conversation, Milt?"

"Do you believe we are?"

"Yes. I do."

"Then we are."

"Was dying hard, Milt?"

"It certainly can be for the body. My death was spectacular, noisy. The men who witnessed it will always see it in their heads from time to time as long as they live."

"Did you die right away?"

"I did. In a flash and an instant. Poof!"

"Do you know when I'll die, Milt?"

"No."

"You're being honest with me?"

"It's not possible for me to be anything else."

"Is heaven nice?"

"It is what it is. You'll see, Billy Ray."

Billy Ray walked back down the ridge, and when he turned around Milt was no longer following him. And really, he didn't think he would run into him again for a lifetime.

# 27

# Home Before Christmas

A light snow fell as Billy Ray boarded the idling train in Memphis. The flakes were wet and sloppy, and the air was very cold and still. The City of New Orleans abruptly hissed and snorted steam, impatient to begin the long journey north. Passengers jammed aisles clutching gifts for Christmas, just days away. Billy Ray had bought a sweater—turquoise with imitation pearl beads woven around the crew collar—for his mother, and assorted striped ties for his father, who Billy Ray knew would grunt and nod and forget their origin rather quickly. The gifts were tucked into Milt's old duffel bag along with his few clothes and the framed picture of Milt that Taylor gave him. Traveling light had become his custom.

He turned on the steps for one last look at Taylor, who tried his best to smile. Billy Ray hovered on the metal steps and gripped the handrail as passengers filed on beside him. He thought that Taylor looked sad and might have jumped aboard, too, if Billy Ray suggested it.

"You'll be home before Christmas," Taylor said. "Tell your ma we're all fine."

"I will, man. Don't do anything with snakes I wouldn't do."

Taylor snickered and jammed his hands in his pockets against the cold. "That's a good one, Billy Ray. Merry Christmas."

"Merry Christmas."

They just stared at each other a moment, grinning, not really sure how best to say goodbye.

"I reckon it's snowing back in Argus, too, Billy Ray."

"I reckon so. That's why they call it winter."

"Good name for it. That way they don't get it mixed up with summer."

"There's not much confusion about that," Billy Ray said.

"Not much reason to go, is there, Billy Ray, if the weather's the same?"

"I have to, Taylor. It's time."

"I know. Did you see everything you needed to see?"

"Yeah, I did."

"Milt?"

"He's in good hands now, Taylor."

Billy Ray eased down to the first step and they shook hands again.

"You'll be back," Taylor said. "Won't you, Billy Ray?"

Billy Ray shot Taylor a crisp salute, one that would have made Milt proud.

"You never know."

He lugged the duffel bag up the steps.

"Hey," Taylor yelled. "Hey, Billy Ray."

Billy Ray re-appeared.

"What did you wish for, Billy Ray?"

"What?"

"On your birthday—what did you wish for?"

Billy Ray thought a moment. Passengers jostled him as they clambered aboard. A porter signaled politely for him to come inside.

"Perspective, man. I wished for perspective."

"Far out, Billy Ray. I hope you find it."

Billy Ray grinned, made a peace sign, and disappeared into the train. At the first window he came to, he waved one more time to Taylor.

The City of New Orleans lurched into motion. Billy Ray was relieved to be under way. He allowed himself to relax and sink into his seat by the window. It was more comfortable than he expected. The atmosphere in his car seemed festive—electric. It was only the second time he had ever been on a train. He looked out the window to see if Taylor was still on the boarding platform, but no one was there and the snow seemed to be coming down faster and thicker.

He wasn't sure how far he'd gone before he could say he was having specific thoughts, and even those were just a jumble of the most recent—the drive to Memphis in Taylor's pickup and the teasing banter. He looked out the window. Memphis was far behind.

The country was open and clear of civilization except for occasional clumps of houses.

Thick stands of forest dotted the landscape. The snow had stopped. He wished he'd bought a map at the station so he could follow the train's progress. He liked to know where he was.

Billy Ray reached deep into the duffel bag, felt the box packed under the Christmas gifts—the gift to himself. It made him laugh out loud, and a young girl sitting across the aisle with her parents heard him and made a funny face and then laughed, too. Billy Ray smiled back, and the girl held up her doll for him to inspect. After a while a porter collected his ticket and then Billy Ray listened to the rhythmic clacking of the rails until it dulled him into an almost dreamless sleep.

Billy Ray woke up with his face pressed into the glass of the window. The sun had come out and warmed his forehead. He sat up and stretched. The little girl and her parents were gone. Looking out the window, he noted that there was more snow on the ground than in Memphis. He sensed that Illinois must be close. It wasn't so far from Memphis to the southern tip of Illinois. He went to the men's room and washed his face and combed his hair, which had grown nearly to his shoulders. The face in the mirror smiled back at him, but he wondered if his father would recognize it. The face seemed a little new to Billy Ray, too.

He went back to his seat and tried to read a Memphis newspaper the porter had offered him, but he couldn't focus enough to read past headlines. He walked back to the club car and ate a pastrami on rye, then watched people's faces a while. He found that he liked traveling by train. Compared to a bus it was like a rolling community that had brought along its own kitchen.

He went back to his seat and wondered what he would say when he got to Champaign and saw his parents. He knew he looked different and wondered if they would seem different to him. He had been gone a long time. It seemed longer to him than it really was. When he thought about those first days on the way to Helena it seemed almost like something he'd heard about, but had not really experienced.

The train slowed to pass through a small town south of Effingham, and Billy Ray saw people on the station platform and streets and in cars and wondered what their lives were like. Would some of them live their entire lives there without ever leaving? What made people accept the boundaries of a small town without complaint—even with pleasure? And how many felt a little trapped, or even caged, sometimes, as he had in Argus? And would Argus seem different? Smaller? Bigger? Would he feel like a stranger, or would he blend back in as though he'd never left?

He napped intermittently. When he was finally awake for good, he felt quite alert and recognized the names of all the towns and knew he would be in Champaign soon. He tried to picture his parents waiting for him, and then the short drive back to Argus along narrow roads once they left the main highway west, but only his mother would come into clear focus. He knew she would wave and smile and point. His father was a fuzzy image, almost a stick man. Some things, he knew, had no solutions—just accommodations. With some people, even family, it was an uneasy alliance at best.

The snow was thick on the prairie outside his window. A flat white ocean as far as he could see. Tiny wisps of smoke curled lazily from the stacks of farmhouses. A low ridge appeared, dotted with clumps of trees, and it made Billy Ray think of surfers on the crest of a wave, waiting to make their runs. He could still go there, to California. Or back to Helena and learn the blues with Tyler Jones. Or Tahiti, for that matter. It was now just a matter of going.

The train slowed, and the porter announced they were coming into the station at Champaign.

Billy Ray felt relief and smiled. He was excited to be almost home. Where he went next was something that would work itself out in time. For now he was pleased to be back and to discover what sort of magic he might work there. He reached into the duffel bag and pulled out the box. The symbol of his new freedom. Billy Ray slipped off his tennis shoes and eased his feet effortlessly into a shiny new pair of Beatle Boots.

# 28

# All the Way Home

The streets of the Argus town square were nearly deserted. All the shops had been closed since ten, and only a few cars were parked outside the VFW across the street, where lights still glowed from the bar. Billy Ray saw a man step outside and light a cigarette, and the blue smoke drifted up to an overhead light. An April moon shone full and it was still very cool, the spring quite shy and not yet willing to make an appearance. Billy Ray could see his breath, but he did not really feel cold. He had pulled up his jacket collar and plunged his hands in his pockets and kept walking toward home, enjoying the crisp air and silence and the intermittent breeze rustling leaves in the trees. Behind him the great clock on the square signalled midnight with a subtle, pleasant tone.

Billy Ray walked past his father's store. The display window was full of plumbing contraptions, but they no longer made Billy Ray wince. He looked without really seeing what was there and then smiled and kept walking. They were just inanimate objects—things. Boring things that did not matter to Billy Ray. That was his father's world, not his. His father had finally seemed to accept that. An understanding of sorts had evolved: by summer Billy Ray would take classes at the community college in Bloomington-Normal and work on the loading dock at Fleener Hardware until something else came along. Mayor Sullivan, still a Billy Ray fan, was working on that.

There was even talk of an Argus blues festival. In return, Billy Ray's father would no longer have the sugarplum dreams of Fleener and Son.

And the Beatle Boots had become non-negotiable.

Billy Ray's newfound maturity afforded him some leverage.

At his parents house the mood had become surprisingly pleasant. His mother was happy to hear college was a solid option. Billy Ray had even suggested he might transfer to ISU, or Illinois over in Champaign. His mother no longer pushed medical school—his parents had gained a new respect for Billy Ray based on his year-long odyssey to Helena. They recognized that the baby fat had been shed and that Billy Ray was no longer a child and now had his own ideas. When Billy Ray offered an opinion, his father would actually listen patiently, if also a little painfully—unless it was about Republican politics, of course. Some things were simply not going to change, but they didn't have to because Billy Ray felt he had moved beyond them. They no longer much affected him.

He wasn't sure what he would ultimately do with himself. No specific profession came to mind. He knew he wasn't doctor material. But college sounded like fun, and he liked to learn. Beyond that he had few clues. But he realized he didn't have to know right away. There was time. He would take classes that sounded interesting and see how it went. There was always the option of going back to Helena to work with the radio station and festival, but he just wasn't sure that would ever be anything more than a temporary gig. It was something to ponder.

Time had seemed to slow down for Billy Ray. People sometimes asked him if he was still intent on becoming a surfer, and Billy Ray would grin widely and say, "That would be fun, wouldn't it?" and then thank them for the interest and move on. At Walgreen's one day he quickly thumbed through a copy of *Surfer* magazine, but the pictures of waves didn't move him like before. They were just pictures. He no longer seemed to step onto the page and feel the wet sting of the surf.

Margie Heinrich had finally come back from Lichenstein. He had nearly forgotten about her. Billy Ray saw her one day from a distance, as she left Cameron's with her mother. They seemed to be in a hurry and appeared to be arguing, too. Margie's hair was shorter, duller, and Billy Ray felt that her face had begun to sag a bit. She was not such a beauty after all, he decided. Then came word that she was pregnant, and of all people, Jimmy Lewis was the father. Jimmy Lewis! It was not happy news to her parents, and her father was known to often get drunk on martinis at the country club and rail about "the little common bastard that screwed his way into the family." Billy Ray was even a little shocked to hear that Margie and Jimmy got married and moved to Bloomington. Margie became quite large, and her once lovely face disappeared into a double chin and heavy cheeks, and Billy Ray felt it was pretty funny, but he also felt a little sorry for her—moderately sorry. But she was no longer the golden girl, and Billy Ray wondered what he had seen in her in the first place.

The war in Vietnam had become a daily topic in Argus—everywhere. It was on TV all the time. Billy Ray watched the twittering helicopters lift off with body bags as the rotors flattened the tall sawgrass. Vietnam looked very hot and humid and seemed a bit too primitive to care much about. Why were we even there, he kept asking himself, and he could not come up with an answer. When his father talked about stopping commies before they could spread to America, Billy Ray instinctively felt that was somehow too simplistic, and he would find a way to avoid those conversations. He could not watch this televised war for long because it always made him think of Milt. He knew that college would provide him with a deferment, and he felt that was a very good thing. He did not yet know how he felt about the war.

He only knew for sure that it had claimed Milt. Perhaps that was all he would ever need to know about it. He lacked his father's blind ideology, his blind and misplaced faith that conservatism cured all ills. Once, over corned beef and cabbage at the VFW, he asked his father whether losing Milt was too high a price for the war, and his father had looked away and muttered something about the cost of freedom and liberty and being vigilant—and sacrifice, too. All Billy Ray knew was that the cost indeed seemed very high. He still missed Milt. But he no longer saw Milt's ghost, and he was thankful for that.

As he walked he thought fleetingly of Moss Newbury, now behind bars for a long time to come. He had visited him once when he got back from Helena. Moss had looked rather gray and small and had aged beyond his young years. His face was so much thinner. Billy Ray hoped that he would continue to visit Moss when he could, but he wasn't entirely sure that he would. Some things just weren't destined, he realized sadly.

His old friend The Cushmaker had died the month after Billy Ray got home. Billy Ray managed to see him several times, and they always laughed about meeting President Johnson. Cush had drank and smoked too much for far too long, and it had caught up with him one night, and he had a heart attack at the VFW while regaling pals about his Navy days in the Pacific during the war. Cush had died among friends over drinks and the tall tales he loved to tell. Billy Ray felt it was somehow fitting. The funeral featured a military honor guard.

The VFW flew the flag at half-mast that day, a windy day, and the Stars and Stripes were whipped mercilessly.

Billy Ray liked walking around Argus late at night, when few people would be seen, and he could have a sense of perspective on how the town once was when he was a kid and how it was changing. Some changes were subtle, like a slowly growing realization that there really was a war that affected even tiny Argus. Milt was no longer the only one from Argus who had been killed. Other changes were more noticeable—more kids dressing like hippies in torn, faded, bell-bottom jeans and tie-dyed shirts and even military jackets, and boys growing their hair long—all much to the open dismay of some of the good folks of Argus who preferred time to stand still.

His nightly walks were also an exercise in asserting his new independence, despite living back home temporarily. The late night jaunts were simply evidence that he came and went as he pleased. He wasn't arrogant about that at all—just emphatic that he had his own direction to take. No one questioned him anymore when he went out the door.

He decided to climb Pruitt Hill, which wasn't so much of a climb as a steep walk. But from the modest summit he could survey Argus clumped on the prairie. There were still lights on here, and there and beyond the town he could see the headlights from a few cars out on the lonely interstate. One direction went to Bloomington and the other to Champaign. He suspected he would be going in one of those directions soon enough as his universe once again expanded beyond Argus.

Billy Ray sat there with his hands clutching his knees. The air had a clean smell and the earlier breeze had settled down. The hill had always been a good place to think and try to get perspective and remember things. He remembered the day, not so far in the past, when he and Moss had shot roman candles at houses below the hill. Kid stuff.

That seemed like ages ago. The memory faded quickly. He scanned the town from east to west and enjoyed the twinkling lights. He wondered who was still up and what they were doing. Were they lonely? Couldn't sleep? Or did they just prefer, like Billy Ray, to be awake and to listen and watch when so many were asleep?

Overhead in the clear sky the stars were a vast field of glittering diamonds. Infinity stretched out before him, inviting him. The moon was bright and seemed close enough to touch. After a while he spotted the flashing lights of an airliner, perhaps on its way to Chicago from St. Louis. Soon he saw a second jet. And then a third. He never knew how busy the night sky could be. It was always moving. It was alive. He knew there were satellites, too, that could be seen if one watched long enough, tiny specks seeming to mingle with stars. And out on the interstate traffic seemed to suddenly pick up for a minute, headlight beams dancing and rushing toward each other. Everyone was going somewhere, Billy Ray thought, and he knew he was not that far behind them.

# Michael Loyd Gray

Michael Loyd Gray was born in Jonesboro, Arkansas, but grew up in Champaign, Illinois. He earned an MFA in English from Western Michigan University and has taught at colleges and universities in upstate New York, Michigan, Illinois, Wisconsin, and Texas. He graduated from the University of Illinois with a Journalism degree and was a newspaper staff writer in Arizona and Illinois for ten years, conducting the last interview with novelist Erskine Caldwell.

He is the winner of the 2005 Alligator Juniper Fiction Prize and the 2005 The Writers Place Award for Fiction. Gray's novel *Well Deserved* won the 2008 Sol Books Prose Series Prize. His novel *Not Famous Anymore* was awarded a grant by the Elizabeth George Foundation and has been released by Three Towers Press. He has written a sequel to *Well Deserved* called *The Last Stop*, and another novel called *Blue Sparta*. Recently he finished a novel titled *Fast Eddie*. A lifelong Chicago Bears and Rolling Stones fan, he lives in Kalamazoo, Michigan, and teaches as full-time online English faculty for South University, where he is one of the founding editors of the student literary journal *Asynchronous* and sponsor of an online readings series featuring fiction and poetry.

# Also by Michael Loyd Gray

*Well Deserved*

The folks of Argus, Illinois, from the small-time dealer to the returning Vietnam vet, the townie grocery clerk and the new sheriff, all know what they want out of life, but the paths to their desires are conflicted and unclear. In a narrative with all the clarity and determination of a prophecy, *Well Deserved* chronicles the struggles of these four people as they come to the stark realization that their paths are not solitary, but entwined, and their very lives hinge on one shared moment.

To learn more about
Skywater Publishing Cooperative
and our upcoming releases,
visit us at https://skywaterpub.com
or scan the QR code below.